PORTRAIT OF A GIRL

PORTRAIT OF A GIRL

Mary Williams

Chivers Press • Thorndike Press
Bath, Avon, England   Thorndike, Maine USA

This Large Print edition is published by Chivers Press, England, and by Thorndike Press, USA.

Published in 1995 in the U.K. by arrangement with the author.

Published in 1995 in the U.S. by arrangement with Laurence Pollinger, Ltd.

U.K. Hardcover ISBN 0–7451–2795–9 (Chivers Large Print)
U.K. Softcover ISBN 0–7451–2863–7 (Camden Large Print)
U.S. Softcover ISBN 0–7862–0501–6 (General Series Edition)

The text of this Large Print edition is unabridged.
Other aspects of the book may vary from the original edition.

Set in 16 pt. New Times Roman.

Printed in Great Britain on acid-free paper.

British Library Cataloguing in Publication Data available

Library of Congress Cataloging-in-Publication Data

Williams, Mary, 1903–
    Portrait of a girl / Mary Williams.
        p.   cm.
    ISBN 0–7862–0501–6 (lg. print : lsc)
    I. Title.
[PR6073.I4323P67   1995]
823′.914—dc20   95–17615

*To the memory of dear Mike,
my husband, whose courage and
enduring love enabled me to carry
on, and write this book.*

CHAPTER ONE

1866

Whenever I think of Kerrysmoor, I see in memory the dark granite shapes of the Three Maidens standing stark against a fading cold sky. In the shadowed valley below, the mansion crouches square-faced beside a wind-driven copse of leafless trees. The vision is only momentary and quickly fades into a veil of drifting fog which finally resolves into something else —the cottage half a mile away that was to bring such beauty and tragedy into my life. Bushes wave in a thin breeze about its doors, swaying rhythmically to the haunted echo of singing.

For a few seconds I am a girl again, caught into the magic and mystery of the past. I see Rupert riding through the fitful light to meet me.

And the pool.

It is still there, but the cottage has become an empty shell, and Kerrysmoor is no more.

A wave of chill suddenly floods me; then just as quickly it is gone, and I am real again, in a present I thought at times could never be.

The beginning of it all was so different. I had my ambitions, from an early age but they were the glittering fantastic dreams of childhood only—of riding like a princess in a shining chaise drawn by white-plumed horses through cheering crowds. 'Princess'—that's what my father called me. He was a Breton seaman and each time he returned home to Falmouth from weeks—sometimes months—away, he brought gifts of silk and wonderful shawls and we'd have a 'dressing up' time while he pinned my hair high with fancy shining combs and ribbons and he would say, '*Ah!—c'est magnifique!*—a real princess.' In time, although my real name was Josephine, I was always Princess to him, which made his wife jealous. She was the daughter of a tavern keeper in Falmouth's docklands where we lived. Anna, who was good-looking in a fierce bold way, liked attention only for herself. There was little sympathy between us, which perhaps was understandable, as she was really only my stepmother. My own mother had died when I was three years old, and Pierre had married Anna twelve months later.

So when he was drowned at sea, I was left, by blood, an orphan, and felt very much alone. I think Anna did her best at first to care for me. But she was over-fond of men, and during my father's absence had been forever in the bar. Consequently I spent hours as a child wandering about the maze of fashionably cobbled streets round Falmouth's harbour, or hiding in corners and round the door of the taproom, listening to bawdy jokes and

2

laughter, and strange chatter in foreign tongues. There was music and singing. Sometimes even I caught the echo of a Celtic melody heard in babyhood, and then I hummed it myself, softly at first, until a strange longing for something unknown and far away filled me. Forgetting caution, and as my voice swelled, I danced, impelled by instinct and a blurred memory of my mother's face—dark-eyed and pale, with her dusky hair blown wild and free as clouds over the Cornish sea. She had been Welsh and '*très belle*', Pierre often told me. Anna had hated him saying it, and once he'd set sail again on a long journey, she'd remarked cruelly; '*Belle!* that means "beauty". And "Princess". Forget it. A little Froggie *you* are—no more. So don't go getting fine ideas. There's only work ahead for you, my girl. And plenty of it.'

Six weeks later we learned that his ship had foundered off the African coast, taking all hands with it.

He was dead.

The next few years were sordid in many ways, holding, however, a strange colourful side that gradually absorbed me by its demimonde atmosphere of dark excitement. I could sing; and as time passed my voice sweetened and matured. While Anna sank further and further into debauchery and shame, I spent many of the night hours entertaining clients of the district's numerous

3

hostelries and inns, by songs and ballads remembered from childhood. In this way I earned sufficient casual money to have occasional good meals and buy shoes, combs and other etceteras to wear with the silk shawls brought for me in the past from overseas by my Breton father.

My looks, also, caught men's attention. I was very pale-skinned, but with a wealth of black hair and eyes of deep dark blue, fringed by thick lashes. When I stared at myself through the mirror occasionally, chin up-tilted, with a little smile on my full lips, I knew why my father had called me 'Princess', and when I sang, I really became one. The dusty interiors of tap rooms and inns disappeared, taking the smell of spirits and bawdy laughter with them, and I was singing—singing—to far away regions of enchantment—of mountains and rivers and eternal springtime. There was sadness too, of dying and being born again! Oh, I never wanted my singing to end; it was as though only through my voice I could really be myself.

Pierre's Princess.

Feeling so made me proud. I allowed no liberties, no man to touch me. Their admiration flattered me, and one day I thought, perhaps someone with influence—some musician or opera producer—might be induced to launch me on the stage to a wider audience. The idea was just a wild dream of those early years, but it was sufficiently vivid and inspiring to keep my life apart from Anna's influence. Occasionally, when she was at her lowest ebb and I had had a particularly successful period singing at some respectable hostelry, I helped her a little financially; in a way I was sorry for her. The inn had become a place of ill-fame, and she had turned into nothing more than a slatternly promiscuous harridan available for any man who wanted her. Her father, who lived drunkenly in an upstairs room, died from a stroke, and soon afterwards Anna herself was found with her throat cut in a dark alley leading from the docks.

Her murderer was never found. The police didn't bother much. Her death was no loss. Only I attended her sordid funeral, and though I tried to feel grief, no tears came—merely a sense of gratitude that Pierre had never known her degradation.

I left that particular district soon after the event, and moved to a more respectable area, where the clientele of the various inns and eating houses had a more restrained and cultured character. My voice soon became appreciated, and my appearances in demand. It was wonderful knowing I could sing, and sing, without lascivious hands wishing to touch me or fondle me. Money too was good. I no longer had to accept what was thrown or meanly afforded.

At the Golden Bird, an establishment frequented by travellers and moneyed people, I was eventually given employment on the regular basis of two hour nightly sessions each evening, for which I was paid quite a handsome sum, and allowed sleeping quarters for myself. My looks and voice still blossomed. I became a symbol for the inn and was soon known as 'the Bird'. Oh, I was happy for those first few months; then gradually a deep longing flooded me for wider spheres and audiences. Singing had become my life. But there were other things too, an awakening emotional hunger of which my voice was only a part.

I was just sixteen when I first met Rupert Verne. It was his eyes that arrested my attention. They were long slits of smouldering deepest gold, unswerving in their gaze, under heavy brows and a wide forehead from which crisp, thick hair waved back. In that first moment of awareness between us I felt excitement flood my veins with a passionate desire that he should know the best of me—the wildest part perhaps—but sense the magic of my songs and share the far-away dreams born in me of my Welsh mother and her love for Pierre my father.

Written down this may sound naive and childish. To Rupert I suppose I could have *seemed* almost a child, with my flying hair and satin skirt swirling beneath the yellow shawl. But my throat had never before arched so joyously, or music trilled so sweetly from it as I lifted my arms above and towards the grouped heads before me. Faces had dimmed and become only blurred discs intermingled with smoke and the fragrance of perfumes and spirits; Rupert's eyes alone glowed, bright with vitality and fire—eyes that never left my face and that I knew must somehow have great significance in my life.

As my song ended he got up. I half believed that he'd make his way between the tables and come towards me. But he didn't. He stood quite still for a moment, watching me, and then turned and slowly, deliberately went away.

Others applauded, and would have crowded round me, but I was so heavy with disappointment, I rushed from the lounge past the taproom to my own humble apartment.

Why had he gone so quickly I wondered? Why had he left without a single word of appreciation? Perhaps after all my singing hadn't really pleased him. He was not exactly a young man—probably in the late thirties—with considerable experience of the Opera. Yet his eyes!—I couldn't forget them, or the way they'd seemed to drain my very spirit from me.

The next night he was there again, alone at a small table with a glass of wine in his hand. The glow of a lantern from an alcove gave the fawn velvet coat he wore the lustre of satin. Everything about him, though of quite good taste, marked him as a man of quality. Yet beneath the civilized facade I sensed emotional undercurrents as tumultuous as my own.

Still he didn't approach me, but as my singing session ended, moved quietly away into the dusk outside. I watched him through the window, place his tall beaver hat on his head, then without another glance at the inn mount the step of a waiting carriage.

Joe Burns, the landlord of the Golden Bird, must have noticed my concentration. He touched my arm in a friendly way and said, 'No use having a fancy for that one, girl—A real gentleman he is, an' with a fine lady wife into the bargain. Verne, his name is—Mr Rupert Verne. Got a large estate on the North Coast. So there's nothin' there for'ee. Now young Harry Bolson—'

I shrugged, snapped my fingers, and said contemptuously, '*Bolson!*—he's not my kind, and your Mr Verne doesn't interest me. No man does.' I could hear my earrings tinkle as I tossed my head.

Joe Burns regarded me solemnly for a moment then turned away and said, 'That's all right by me, girl. There's always work for you here. As a matter of fact, I was thinking of raisin' your wage again.'

He kept to his word; I should have been content, but I wasn't, simply because for seven whole evenings Mr Rupert Verne didn't appear again. I supposed during the interim he'd become bored with my entertainment and had found something more stimulating—perhaps even returned to the vast estate I'd been told of in North Cornwall.

Oh well, I decided defiantly, so be it. There were other, more youthful, male faces to admire me. At the end of the week therefore, being in a coquettish mood, I donned a particularly gay attire of an orange-coloured swirling skirt over a peacock-blue silk shawl, and with a poppy behind one ear, above a jingling earring, broke into a medley of French songs, dancing to the rhythm of an Apache number. How my feet pirouetted, how my arms swayed and my thick dark curls flew to the melody, and oh!—how wonderful it was when the door at the far end of the taproom opened revealing the square-shouldered figure of Rupert Verne impressively silhouetted against the glow of the swinging oil lamp outside.

He was wearing a caped coat, and as he entered swung his stove hat from his head. The light's rays lit the chestnut hair and lean carved lines of his face to orange fire. Something electric in the atmosphere caused heads to turn. Movement ceased, mugs and bottles were momentarily stilled. No sound any more came from my throat. My slippers were motionless on the floor.

Then, suddenly, he strode forward, and said for all to hear, 'I beg no pardon for the intrusion, but ask your co-operation. This young lady and myself have matters of some importance to discuss, and I've had a hard ride, so for your deprivation of the night's pleasure—allow me—!'

He flung a fistful of coins into the gathering, quickened his approach to me and took the tips of my fingers for a second in his, then led me into the shadowed back portion of the inn.

I was bemused and exhilarated at the same time; it was as though a strange kind of enchantment had fallen upon me. The door of the back parlour opened slightly—through a chink of light I saw Joe Burns' face watching curiously. At a quick glance from Mr Verne the latch snapped, and we were alone in the fusty room. I stood with my head raised, fiddling with the fringe of shawl drawn close to my neck. There was a brief pause in which the monotonous sound of an ancient carved mahogony clock ticked the moments away. It was a drab brown room that badly needed dusting. An oleograph of the Battle of Trafalgar hung on the wall, a tired potted plant drooped on the sill, yellow and sick-looking in the wan lamplight. Embers in the fireplace were already dying, and remains of a meal had been left on the table. I was aware of these things, but they held no meaning for me. My heart was beating wildly. Every sense in me was heightened and expectant.

I waited.

Through the film of blurred air I watched the

golden slits of eyes widen, and a faint smile pucker his lips. Then he spoke. 'Don't be afraid. I've no foul designs on you.'

Beneath the shawl I could feel my flesh burn, and felt a warm glow flood my cheeks. Words came from my lips mechanically. 'Of course not. Why should you?'

His whole body relaxed. 'Sit down,' he said. 'We may as well be comfortable. I have a proposition to put to you.'

I obeyed, waiting for him to take a seat, but he didn't, he just perched himself on the edge of the table and continued, 'Don't you want to know what it is?'

Already aware of the designs of most men, I managed to answer a little haughtily, 'I'm not sure, sir. I may be young but I've had propositions before.'

His voice hardened. 'Not of this kind. I'm not lusting after your luscious pretty body or any feminine favours. In other words, child, I'm a married man with no taste for affairs on the sly—'

'I—'

He raised a hand from which an emerald flashed its green fire. 'Now don't argue, if you please. You have a voice. Looks, too, of course, of a wild kind, but it is your voice I—covet.'

'Why? What for?'

'Ah. That's better. What for? To have trained—to bring it to its full potential. Do you understand?'

When I shook my head mutely, he resumed. 'You should have wider audiences than those in hostelries and taverns. I can make no promises of course—but I'm pretty certain that after a period of tuition you would be welcome on the best concert stages of Cornwall and the West—later perhaps through the whole land. You'd have to work hard and accept strict discipline, naturally, but luckily I happen to have friends in the theatre world—and the man I have in mind lives now not too far away— retired—near Truro. I'm quite sure he'd be delighted to undertake your tuition, if you're willing and agree to my plans—' His voice broke off.

I simply stared. Although I'd long dreamed of the opportunity offered, I hadn't really expected it to materialise. I could feel my heart bumping wildly, then miss a beat or two as the blood rushed to my face before receding to leave me trembling. Damp curls clung to my forehead. This was all I had longed for, and more, much more—simply because Rupert Verne himself was concerned. That he was older than me—nearer forty than thirty, married, with a wife and owner of a large estate—that he had wealth and position, didn't in those first ecstatic moments register. A bond, a promise, had already been forged between us. Whatever happened in the future I knew that in some strange way we were already bound, for good or ill.

'Well?' I heard him say, through the dizzy whirl of excitement. 'Are you dumb, child? Or just not interested?'

'Of course I'm interested,' I heard myself reply, almost in a whisper. 'Of course. Of course—'

He smiled, and touched my shoulder lightly. It could have been a fatherly touch; but it wasn't—quite. For a second or two the years between us were dispelled. The whole world seemed to brighten and sing. We stood—woman and man facing each other on an enchanted shore while knowledge flowered and I knew life would never be quite the same again. Then, suddenly, it was over. Facts came into focus. I was merely Josephine Lebrun, a girl possessing a voice good enough to stir the interest of a would-be wealthy sponsor. So I steeled myself to appear dignified, even a little aloof, and continued, though still breathlessly, 'Who is he? This theatre person? And how do you know I'd please him?'

'I don't. We shall have to find out.'

The sudden abrupt tone of voice and manner chilled me. It was as though in a few short words he deliberately intended to cast me down.

Perhaps I'd been stupid and taken too much for granted. Perhaps after all, this idea of his was a mere whim—a rich man's passing game to provide stimulus and amusement for a time.

Or perhaps he really was genuine, but cautious of disappointing me. The uncertainty must have shown in my expression. I felt my shoulders droop as I got up and turned towards the door. In a second he was there before me.

'Now don't you run away,' I heard him saying, as though talking to a child. 'You must learn not to show moods or tempers. And don't expect praise all the time. You have a nice voice, yes. But Signor Luigi will expect more than that—'

'Luigi?'

'My friend. He is half Italian, and was once a famous name in Opera—as a tenor in his prime, and later as producer. So of course, his contacts are valuable. If he thinks your talent worth troubling about I've no doubt I'll be able to persuade him to take you on. But you'll have to obey him and work hard. He can be a difficult tutor, because he is naturally a perfectionist. Do you understand? Have you the first idea of what I'm trying to din into you?'

The golden slits of his eyes gleamed brilliantly, unswervingly on mine.

With my chin lifted an inch higher I faced him very directly.

'I think so. I'm trying.'

'Very well. This then is what I propose. You will leave the Golden Bird in the next few days, and travel with me to my home on the North

14

Coast. There is a cottage on the estate where you can live providing you keep an eye on certain things. I have a caretaker there, but she is getting old and not entirely capable of handling special *objets d'art*. Her eyes are no longer very good, and her hands are shaky, but she can cook still, and do a certain amount of cleaning. If you are willing you will assist her when necessary, for your board and lodging, and of course to help pay for your tuition. Luigi does not give his services for nothing.'

He paused; and after a moment I asked, 'Where, if I agree, shall I have my lessons? There? At your cottage?'

He gave a short laugh.

'My dear girl! no, of course not. Once or twice a week my chaise will take you to Truro. Your lessons can be arranged for suitable premises according to Luigi's choice. That is—if he agrees.'

If—*if*! again the doubt.

Although exhilarated still, I was bewildered, a little uneasy. Everything had happened so quickly, and I couldn't help wishing that the future could have been arranged without the necessity of having to be dictated to by the 'perfectionist'—the critical and, I was sure, fiery Italian Luigi.

Apart from that the condition that I'd be expected to help at the cottage in any caretaking business seemed a little strange. I didn't much like the idea of being confined in a

15

small cottage with a shaky old woman whose faculties were failing. Did it mean that I'd hardly ever see Rupert Verne? I had no *right* to, of course. I must remember that always. He was married. His interest in me was supposedly because of my voice only. So if I really co-operated with his plan I must severely control all emotional impulses. Only through my singing would my heart be free to express the hunger and joy of living.

Therefore, I forced myself to appear more calm and dignified, and the result of that propitious interview was that the following week I set off with Mr Rupert Verne in his chaise for Kerrysmoor.

We travelled cross-country over a high moorland route up and down brown hills, past grey farms and villages, and bleak hamlets of miners' cottages huddled along the coast. The wild horizon of earth and sky was dotted intermittently by dolmens, standing stones, and the rhythmic movement of tin-mine pumping rods smokily dark in the yellowing autumn evening. Occasionally the winding road curved close to giant cliffs bordering the sea. Through the clip clop of horses' hooves and rattle of wheels the thunderous pounding of waves could be heard menacingly crashing against jutting rocks hundreds of feet below.

Mr Verne was silent for most of the way. The coldness of the landscape began to oppress me. For the last few miles we passed no living

16

creature but a few cows and sheep huddled in stone-walled fields, and a pedlar's cart pulled by a donkey driven by a hunched brown-skinned man. He wore a woollen cap with a feather in it, and touched it as the vehicle passed by. Rupert Verne gave a slight inclination of his head. I glanced at him enquiringly.

'Tammy Vicks the pedlar,' Rupert said casually, adding with a hint of humour in his voice though no smile touched his lips. 'A much respected man hereabouts—Tammy.'

'Oh.'

'Heard of pellars?'

'No,' I replied. 'Pedlars, yes. But pellar—'

'Almost the same thing. Both go about selling things. But a true pellar is also a conjurer said to possess magic powers and cures for healing.'

I stared at him. 'Do *you* believe that, sir?'

'What *I* believe is of no account,' he answered shortly.

'I see.' I felt snubbed and must have shown it, for he continued after a short pause, 'I accept what I know to be fact and take the rest with a pinch of salt. You'll hear many strange stories round here—myths and legends grown from ancient times. Take them as such. Remember the reason you've come to Kerrysmoor. Your voice.'

'I hope you won't be disappointed.'

'So do I, for your own sake.'

His stiff words sent a wave of resentment through me.

'I could always return to Falmouth. Mr Burns was satisfied. I brought him good custom,' I said sharply.

'Did you indeed?' Conscious that he had turned his head quickly to look at me, I kept my chin up, and eyes fixed straight ahead.

'Yes,' I heard him continue, still in the same abrupt stilted tones, 'I can well believe it. You have a piquant air.'

That was not what I'd wished him to say. Not the type of compliment I'd expected when I recalled the intense interest of those strange amber eyes as they'd first rested on me in the taproom of the Golden Bird. Sudden chill filled me; not only because of my deflated mood, but because freshened with the fading of daylight, drifts of cool air penetrated the interior of the chaise in damp waves of rising mist.

I pulled my cloak more tightly to my chin, and then, as the vehicle rounded a corner of the lane I saw the house hunched square and dark against the shape of a rising hill. Through the uncertain light no details of style or architecture were visible. To one side a copse of trees blew in a thin wind. The rest of the valley was in shadow, but the rim of moor above was starkly clear against the greenish glow of fading twilight, topped by three tall standing stones. My heart, for a second, seemed to miss a beat, because it seemed to me that as the

18

chaise drew nearer to the drive, they appeared to lurch forward of their own volition.

Mr Verne must have noticed. He gave a short laugh. 'The Three Maidens,' he said. 'Quite dramatic at certain times of day. Not that you'll have time to go wandering that way. Tonight you'll stay at Kerrysmoor, but tomorrow you'll be driven to the cottage— Tregonnis, and quite soon I shall arrange a meeting for you with your tutor.'

Such was my introduction to a whole new phase of my life which was to hold such disaster, tragedy, and periods of overwhelming joy.

*   *   *

The interior of the house depressed me on that first evening. The lighting from various lamps was insufficient to penetrate the gloom of winding corridors and dark recesses where shadows flickered eerily over black-framed, ancient portraits, giving a curious impression of life.

An elderly woman wearing a mob cap and apron over a starched, dark dress greeted me grudgingly, and was introduced by Mr Verne as Mrs Treen, the housekeeper. She nodded curtly, saying, 'Follow me. Your room's this way.'

I glanced at Mr Verne; his face was expressionless. He was waiting obviously for

19

me to obey, which I did. The hall was flagged, covered at intervals by rugs. Half way down we passed a wide staircase leading up from the right. It curved sharply in a bend beneath a Gothic-style stained-glass window, and for a moment a brilliant shaft of lighting from above threw a static figure into vivid clarity. The form was that of a woman—elegantly thin and wearing a purple wrap. Her face was deadly pale under the intensely black piled-up hair. She held a lamp in one hand, and stood so still and watchful I was discomforted, sensing no welcome or warmth from her—only critical resentment.

'Come along, girl,' I heard Mrs Treen say. 'We haven't all the time in the world.' Rupert Verne moved away, and at the same time the woman turned and retreated round the bend into the shadows. A faint soughing of wind and tree tapping against the window merged into the rustle of silk skirts and softly dying footsteps.

'Who was that?' I had the temerity to ask. 'On the stairs.'

'It isn't really your business,' came the reply tartly. 'But as you're leaving tomorrow, and there's no mystery about Madam's presence I'll tell you—for your own good. The lady on the stairs was Mr Rupert's wife, Lady Alicia. She's the daughter of a very noble house, and much respected. So if you happen to meet before your departure you'd better remember

20

your manners.'

I wanted to retort indignantly that I did not come from the gutter, and knew how to behave in the presence of gentry, but was wise enough to keep the words back. After all, entertaining well-bred pleasure seekers in respectable hostelries like the Golden Bird had demanded quite a different code of behaviour than bowing to her ladyship. No curtseying or minding one's words—just smiling and dancing, and singing for the joy of it. Depression enfolded me in a grey cloud. For the first time I doubted the wisdom of having left Falmouth for the grim atmosphere of Kerrysmoor.

In the morning, though, optimism had returned. When I jumped out of bed and pulled the window curtains wide, pearly sunlight touched distant cliffs to gold. The sea beyond was calm under a lifting cloudless sky. Immediately below the wall of the house, terraced gardens sloped to an expanse of moor where gorse flamed between clumps of purple heather and burnished undergrowth. Any memory of the steep hill behind surmounted by the gloomy Three Maidens was dispelled.

'I shall like it here,' I thought, forgetting for a moment that in an hour or two, perhaps less, I should be leaving for the unknown destination of Tregonnis.

I had breakfast on my own in a small back parlour off the kitchen, consisting of gruel and

21

a slice of thick ham. The master, I was told, had already eaten and her ladyship never rose until noon, taking little refreshment before the midday meal for which she was usually joined by Mr Verne in the dining room.

'The mistress isn't well today,' Mrs Treen told me, a little smugly, I thought, 'so 'tisn't likely you'll meet before you leave.'

I was slightly disappointed—not by missing any direct encounter with the haughty creature glimpsed on the stairs the previous night, but by the silence of the house and apparent shortage of staff. I had expected to see footmen and servants about, but except for a kitchen maid and a boy in shabby livery carrying boots from the scullery, no one appeared. In daylight the interior of Kerrysmoor had a dingy appearance. Walls needed re-decorating and there were gaps in tiled floors showing damp in places. The rugs in the back hall were partially threadbare.

From Joe Burns' description of a wealthy household I had expected spic and span elegance, even in servants' quarters. But sunlight streaming across floors and corners emphasised years of long neglect.

The housekeeper must have sensed my unspoken criticism. 'This place is old and takes a deal of keepin' in order,' she said. 'And large. You haven't seen anything of the proper dwelling quarters, or the West Wing where Lady Alicia has her apartments. Really elegant it is there. Every year sees it done up and something new added. But of course that's only right, seeing who she is.'

'I see,' I replied ineffectually.

She shook her head. 'No, my girl, you don't. 'Tisn't to be expected. Not with your background.'

'What do you mean? You don't know a thing about me.'

'Now, now, don't get all hoity toity! No harm meant. I was only going by your appearance.'

'And what's wrong with it?'

She smiled—not pleasantly—as her small eyes regarded me shrewdly.

'You've a bit of a wild look on you, to me. That black hair and those eyes! And the way you walk and swing your hips! Oh, attractive in a way I s'pose—enough to charm the master. Gipsyish. But—'

Discretion deserted me. 'Do you mind holding your tongue? My father was a sea-captain, Breton. And my mother was Welsh. That's why I'm here—I've inherited it—her voice. Mr Verne heard me perform and has offered to give me training.'

My sudden haughty tone had the effect of quietening her manner—or perhaps it was the unexpected appearance of Rupert Verne— quite unknown to me—in the doorway.

'I meant no offence,' she said. 'You took my words wrongly—'

'I should hope so,' Rupert's voice interrupted cuttingly.

Startled, both of us turned. He was standing motionless there, with the light from the window striking sideways across his lean face, emphasising the stern, tight-lipped set of his mouth and cold fire of his eyes.

'I didn't mean—' Mrs Treen began, but was silenced by a wave of his hand. He came towards us and addressing the housekeeper continued, 'You should know by now that any guest in my household must be treated with respect, Mrs Treen. I'm most displeased; however, this time the incident will be overlooked providing nothing of the kind ever happens again. Josephine—Miss Lebrun—' He glanced at me sharply—

'Yes, sir?'

'It *would* perhaps be more suitable to the occasion now if you changed into quieter attire. In half an hour's time we're setting off for the cottage, and my caretaker there will probably expect her new companion to appear less flamboyant.'

I should have felt snubbed if it had not been for the unexpected glint of amusement in his glance.

'Very well,' I said. 'I'm sorry.'

He shrugged. 'No need to be. I'm sure Signor Luigi will appreciate a taste of colour providing your voice also charms his artistic heart.'

So I left him with Mrs Treen and went upstairs to the bedroom where I had a black shawl and skirt, and a dark cape to cover everything. I took the rings from my ears, and tied my hair back before pinning it to the top of my head. Over this I placed a small bonnet trimmed only by two flat velvet flowers. It had ribbons to tie under the chin, and the whole effect, when I was dressed, made me suddenly want to giggle. I could have been some young Breton housewife attired primly for a shopping expedition to market.

However, Mr Verne made no comment when I went down later carrying my small valise, ready for the journey. No glance from his eyes even denoted approval or the reverse. I was disappointed, but determined not to show it. If he wished now to have things on an entirely impersonal and business-like basis then I'd prove I was quite capable of obliging.

We spoke little during the journey. The lane curved round the base of a high moorland hill on one side, with a narrow thread of river on the other. The morning air was pungent with the damp smell of mist, fallen leaves and blackberries, and decaying vegetation. Far to the west silvered sunlight lit the distant sea. But the glimpse was soon lost as the chaise turned abruptly inland to the left. The trees bordering the lane thickened; dew diamonded their lean dark branches, giving an air of mystery and enchantment. Everything was very still—the

25

hollow sound of hooves and wheels reverberated weirdly through the windless air. I lifted my hand once to clear the smudged glass of a window.

'There's not much to see yet,' Mr Verne said. 'By midday when the fog's lifted you'll find the view more hospitable. I must see some of these trees are cut down.'

'Are we still on your estate then, sir?' I asked.

'Not really. The cottage is on Kerrysmoor land. As the crow flies—if we had wings—' he continued, 'we could be there in next to no time at all. This hill is Rosecarrion; we're bending back now towards the area from where we started.'

'Oh.' I tried to get an accurate picture in my mind of the locality. 'Then isn't it possible to go the other way, or over the hill?'

'There's no road fit for a carriage of any kind on the other side,' he answered, 'and crossing the hill would be not only difficult, but quite dangerous.'

'Dangerous?'

'Bog, and mine shafts—also adders,' I was told. 'I don't advise you to take any future rambles directly up Rosecarrion.' He glanced in the opposite direction where a humped bridge crossed the river. 'If you go that way you'll discover pleasant paths leading to Tharne. Tharne, though only a small village, is comparatively civilised, and even has a stores where I'm sure you'd find pleasing varieties and most things women want.'

I didn't answer. The mere fact that he'd done his best to put me off wandering about the wild hill had stimulated a wish in me to do so. I was used to going my own way; I suppose it was an instinct born in me through my Celtic and Breton ancestry. To be referred to in the category of 'most women' was mildly irritating. Freedom was in my very blood. I bit my lip momentarily, then relaxed, realising that in the future I would most certainly have to discipline myself to certain rules and regulations.

Round a sudden corner of the hill the lane branched off to the left into what was little more than a track. Long shadows now showed only a thread-like glimmer of light. The coach took the bend, carefully at a slow speed under drooping trees. Evening had deepened so swiftly it could have been almost night. Then as the trunks of oak, sycamore, larch and willow thinned, a shaft of light zig-zagged down the path, revealing a cottage tucked behind a square of garden, with a mellow glow streaming from a half open door.

The chaise drew up nearby; there was the whinnying of horses, and Rupert Verne's voice saying, 'Here we are. Tregonnis.'

He got up, and as he helped me from the vehicle the figure of an old lady appeared coming towards us down the path. She was thin, small, a little bent at the shoulders, but agile in movement, and strangely dressed in old-fashioned attire, wearing a frilled lace cap and apron, a hooped black silk dress spattered with sparkling jewels and brooches. Under the glow of an oil lamp already lighted in the hall I saw the tips of red satin slippers peeping beneath her skirts. She had red ribbons also at her wrists and decorating her hemline in tiny rosettes. Rings glittered from fingers of both hands. Her face was thin and pale with a pointed chin and high-bridged nose.

Mr Verne introduced her as Dame Jenny Trenoweth, 'keeper of Tregonnis', and I as his temporary ward who would be for the time being in her charge, and to give help when necessary. Obviously, she had been well primed concerning my stay at the cottage and the true purpose of it. She expressed no surprise, but nodded all the time he was speaking, her small bright eyes regarding me shrewdly and unblinkingly.

Having expected to find someone more of Mrs Treen's type, I was bewildered by this first glimpse of the quaint creature who appeared more suited to be a character in a play than in real life. Her voice, too, was light and high, but I guessed could be sharp if she felt like it.

Conversation between the three of us was short. Indeed after the first introduction and intimating of my expected behaviour and duties, Rupert Verne appeared anxious to leave.

'The horses will be getting restless,' he said. 'The light's bad, and my wife likes dinner to be punctual. First, though, I would like to show you my—collection. Dame Jenny has been its previous guardian for many years. In future you will share the duty. Dame Trenoweth—' he indicated the parlour door with a wave of his hand, 'you first please, and we'll follow.'

The red slippers made a tapping noise, the necklaces and silk dress tinkled and rustled as the tiny figure led us through the hall to a door on the right, further down. The surround was arched, and the wood, of light oak, was panelled and carved in a symbolic and intricate design. From a pochette hanging at her wrist Dame Jenny took a bunch of keys, she inserted one in the lock, and we went into the room. It was larger than I'd expected, and at some time in the past, obviously, had been converted from perhaps two smaller ones of plain architecture into an interior of intriguing nooks and alcoves.

Candles had already been lighted, throwing fantastic shadows about the treasures stored there—French figurines, music boxes, ivory miniatures in velvet frames, and paintings of exquisite beauty; the walls were silver grey, the ceiling blue and one wall comprised entirely of a large white marble fireplace with settles round it for seating.

It was not possible at first glance to absorb details. The rosy glow of burning logs and candles emphasised the air of mystery and days long ago—countless years in which the treasures must have been collected. There were paintings—mostly water-colours of landscapes that seemed to quiver with life as transient shadows crossed their surface. The delicate poised figure of a glass dancing piper flashed with rainbow movement when I took a step forward, disturbing the quiet air. Then it was stilled again into shadow. I stared round wonderingly, then glanced back again to the fireplace because above it was the focal point of the whole room.

A portrait.

The painting of a girl with upswept silver-pale gold hair tied high with a green ribbon. Her face was heart-shaped from which hazel eyes stared with the translucent quality of moorland pools lit briefly by sunlight. The mouth appeared on the verge of laughter but the whole effect was of longing—the longing and sadness of beauty unfulfilled. I was fascinated, briefly magnetised, sensing that the surroundings were merely a background, perhaps a dedication, to her personality. Above a froth of lace her slim neck held an opalescent glow, ivory pale, yet changeful in the flickering candlelight with all the glowing radiance of waves breaking gently on a cool shore.

Who was she, I wondered? Envy stirred me for a moment, because I felt instinctively she must somehow, in some secret way, hold a place in Rupert Verne's life.

'What a lovely portrait,' I heard myself saying ineffectually.

'Yes.' The one word fell short and curtly from his lips. I glanced at him expectantly. 'Is it anyone—?'

'You'll never meet her,' he interrupted. 'It's just a good painting, and the setting is right. That's why it's there.'

'I see.' But I was disappointed; I felt he could have told me so much more. His expression, I noticed, had tightened. There was a bleak guarded look in his eyes and in the set of his mouth that told me I trod dangerous ground and should stop questioning.

So I said no more on the subject. More practical matters were discussed in which I learned I would not be seeing Signor Luigi until the end of the following week, when the chaise would arrive to take me to Truro.

'Dame Jenny will have time to see that your clothes are in order and suitable for your introduction,' he added before leaving. 'She's an excellent needlewoman, and if anything is required word can be sent to Kerrysmoor. Jan Carne will bring a message.' I wondered who Jan was, but didn't ask.

'That's right,' the old lady said, nodding her head briskly several times. 'These old fingers of mine mayn't be as nimble as they once were, but I can still sew a seam or tuck, and put in a

31

daisy or two when needed.'

Her cheeks had turned very pink; she reminded me of a bedecked robin inquisitively inspecting its domain. I noticed also that her thin ringed hands had a tremor. No wonder Mr Verne no longer considered her quite capable of safely dusting and moving the treasured figurines and curios in the room we'd just left. I had misgivings myself when I considered the responsibilities were in future to be partly mine.

Minutes later Rupert was at the door saying farewell. He held the tall beaver hat in his hand a second before replacing it on his head, turning, and walking briskly away down the path to the waiting chaise. During that brief second his eyes held mine again while excitement churned in me—an electrical awareness of communion binding all the nerves of my body into a hungry fire of desire.

Against my will I made a slight instinctive movement towards him. Did his left hand make a faint gesture of acknowledgement beneath the lace cuff? Just for that fleeting instant did the lines of his stern mouth soften?—the lids quiver over the long golden eyes? I shall never know. My head and senses were whirling so that imagination became confused out of focus with reality.

When my heart had steadied he was already at the gate. A minute afterwards he was ensconced in the chaise, and the vehicle, following a flick of the coachman's whip, was moving down the shadowed lane, throwing a zig-zag of fading light before it, from the swaying lamps.

Evening had faded into deep dusk. When we moved into the hall again Dame Jenny took me up a narrow staircase to my bedroom. The walls were all of white, the furnishings of light oak in an old world style. There was one window overlooking the garden at the back of the cottage. After the old lady had gone I pulled the curtains and looked out. The deep velvet blue sky was already pin-pointed by starlight, but the night was not yet dark enough to obscure the looming shape of the hill rising formidably against it. There was something else too—which I thought at first was probably my imagination. But in the morning I knew my conjecture to be true. Three gaunt shapes stood at a different angle from my first glimpse of them—silhouetted in the morning light.

The Three Maidens.

There was no practical reason why I should have sensed an omen in their presence. But I was filled with momentary, irrational depression. Why? A second later I'd dispelled it. I was, after all, half Welsh, half Breton, which could be the reason for my Celtic mood.

It was the only sensible answer and one I made myself accept.

CHAPTER TWO

During those first few days at Tregonnis, Dame Jenny was completely non-communicative about matters concerning Kerrysmoor or the Verne family, and when I questioned her about the history of the cottage and priceless valuables of the 'treasure room', she became stubbornly silent—almost hostile.

'None of your business, miss,' she said in her thin piping tones. 'All you have to do is help me, as the master said—take down anything that needs dusting so there's no danger of it falling, and polishing—those fancy chairs' legs need attention. 'Tisn't so easy any more for me to bend or get down on my old knees. I keep the key of the room myself. Every morning I take a look round, so see you're about between ten and eleven, an' I'll be able to let thee in.'

'Yes, Dame Jenny,' I agreed meekly.

She nodded, adding, 'You can help me with the baking too. There's an apron in the kitchen to cover all those fancy things you do wear. Then soon as possible we'll get to thinking 'bout what stitching's to be done to make thee presentable for meeting the music man.'

I smiled to myself at her reference to Signor Luigi as 'the music man'.

'Hope you know how to use the needle *properly*,' she added. 'I was always one with a liking for dainty flowers and tucks. But, of course, your cape must be quiet and moderate, I've a piece of brown velvet upstairs might do. No use worrying the master for gold to waste on material when it's there safely folded in my chest upstairs. Still, we'll see 'bout those things a bit later; maybe tomorrow. You take things easily today, girl, get used to the cottage an' garden. Done any prunin' or weedin', have thee?'

I shook my head. 'No. In Falmouth we didn't have a garden.'

'Hm. Well, there'll be bits to do here. But never touch my roses, mind. Roses is delicate things that need dainty handling. With care I have them bloomin' most all the year round. Even at Christmas I've known red buds openin' to cheer the winter.'

When I went out to the back later I discovered that she had in no way exaggerated. On one side of path comprised of pebbles and small rocks of granite quartz reflecting different shades, in the early morning sunlight crimson roses blossomed, mingling colourfully with bronze and gold chrysanthemums.

On the other side, half shadowed by drooping willow, water-lily leaves dappled the surface of a motionless pool. It appeared deep, reflecting the shape of a poised white marble statue at the far end—that of a woman emerging from reeds and ferns, staring into the water. She had one arm over a breast, a bowl or

35

kind of urn held in the other, from which delicate plants trailed. Much of the figure was lost in the verdant undergrowth, but the evasive light gave an uncanny impression of life and momentary movement. The whole effect emanated an emotional quality that affected me oddly.

I tore my eyes from the pool and glared up at the great hill behind. The morning light emphasised the rugged character of the rising moor—great boulders and tumps of heather and gorse, interspersed with the inky grassy darkness of bog and gaping shafts. A derelict mine stack stood halfway down below the Three Maidens. Not a pleasant vista exactly—primitive, intimidating almost, in its wild aloofness, yet challenging, and I knew, despite Rupert Verne's warning, a day would come when I would set out in exploration.

Meanwhile I determined to make every effort at pleasing the quaint keeper of Tregonnis, and managed to acquire a certain amount of trust from her, though her old eyes had a watchful look whenever I strayed beyond the garden gate.

'Ye recall what the master told thee—' she said one day. 'Keep away from the hill. There's plenty of interest in the garden since you like fresh air, and I can teach thee a deal 'bout herbs from my own small patch—it's at the side beyond the roses. There's some bunchings to do before drying—your hands look nimble enough. And what about your voice? I haven't heard any singing yet to speak of—just that humming when you're in the treasure room. There's my fiddle to accompany you when you feel like practising. I was good on the strings in my day.'

I didn't attempt to explain to her that all her fussy restrictions quelled any natural impulse to burst into song, or that her country style of fiddling would only put me off. However, she didn't press the point, but insisted on me putting certain hours of every day into stitching at my 'wardrobe'. The velvet material was used for a cloak-coat with velvet band trimmings. The material was sent to Truro to be cut by a costumier patronised by Lady Verne and sent back to Dame Jenny for making up. This was a tiring business for me, and my day-dress of green silk to be fixed over a moderate bustle, was more so. It had an apron front and white lace collar. There was a good deal of piping to do, and numerous tiny buttons to sew on. Dame Jenny was certainly nimble with her fingers. If she hadn't been I should have been working day and night, because in the past I'd worn mostly colourful shawls to cover hastily converted gowns. Inwardly I fumed and fretted; how much easier and more relaxing it would have been to have taken Rupert Verne's offer of buying clothes from a professional establishment.

I liked the headgear. It was re-styled, hardly

a bonnet, hardly a hat—with small flowers and bows on it, and was a relic from the old lady's chest where she kept precious nick-nacks of her own stowed away. A single white plume curved neatly round the back of the crown, with a shred of veiling floating behind. Tilted precociously forward on my coiled upswept hair it looked quite intriguing. Dame Jenny nodded cautiously when I turned from the mirror to face her.

'It will do, I suppose,' she said one afternoon with a hint of criticism in her voice. 'A little saucy, but then you've that air about you. So long as you do keep your eyes fixed down modest-like we must hope it won't offend. I've heard tell those Italians, singers and such-like, go in for a bit of show. A little rice powder on your cheeks will help make you less—colourful.' Her lips closed primly on the last word.

I laughed; I couldn't help it. Everything—the whole situation, the future, the old lady's grudging admiration and the thought of extending a gloved hand to Signor Luigi like any duchess stirred pleasurable excitement in me. I felt my throat trembling, and without warning joyous notes of solfa rose from my lips, turning involuntarily into a song—a song of mountains and rivers, of far off places and unknown passion luring me to the sweet rich fulfilment of love. I was trilling in the only way I knew—naturally, with abandon. My voice was firm, and full and sweet, realising all the longing I'd felt during the last few weeks for Rupert Verne.

When the sound died and I waited hesitantly with my bosom rising and falling breathlessly under my bodice, there was a prolonged pause from the old lady. She stood simply staring before remarking: 'You certainly have a pair of good lungs, girl. But if you take my advice you'll remember to control them in a ladylike fashion when the time comes to meet the great man. No doubt in low class hostelries, sailors and drinking folk 'ppreciate a deal of show and noise—but any famous acquaintance of the master will expect a taste of refinement.'

'Oh, but I have to sing as I feel,' I told her bluntly. 'Refinement or—or coarseness doesn't come into it. If I had to be controlled and careful there'd be no song—' I broke off with a tinge of doubt rising in me, and it was at that moment the door creaked, sending a wave of cooler air into the parlour.

Startled, I looked round. Mr Verne stood there, top hat in one hand, wearing a black broadcloth cut-away coat with a cape slung over the other arm. His watchful eyes had a concentrated enigmatic look in them, but I fancied there was a tilt of approval round his mouth, and I was once more conscious of his strange sense of power, of an awareness between us that set my pulses leaping with wild restrained joy.

39

'Practising already?' he said in level tones. 'Good. In two days' time we go to meet Signor Luigi.'

'Two days?' I echoed. 'I thought—'

'If you're ready, that is,' he added and turning to Dame Jenny remarked, 'providing the dress-making session permits. At the moment I must say you look—quite charming.'

Dame Jenny appeared slightly flustered.

'If I'd known you were calling today, master, I'd have had things more shipshape. This is only a try on. There be gloves and all manner of little things to 'tend to, and a few alterations. And—' with quite a stern glance at me, 'no more interruptions of tra-la-ing.'

He allowed himself to smile then. 'Oh, I'd call what I heard at the gate more than tra-la-la-ing. Surely *you* with your knowledge of good music must appreciate that, Mrs Trenoweth?'

Mollified, she replied, 'Good music? I'm not all that well versed in such as opera, Master Verne. The fiddle's more to my taste, as it was to my father and his before him. But if you 'ppreciate my young lady's voice then good it must be, I'm sure.'

Shortly after that brief interim of conversation between us, Mr Verne left. There was a further flurry of the dressmaking session, during which I was content to keep silent in case I betrayed my secret feelings to Mrs Trenoweth. Excitement gradually calmed to a deep glowing happiness that held no thought of the past or morrow, or the strange circumstances that had brought me into contact with Rupert. No impossible plans for the future stirred me. He was married, and not the type of man to treat any woman lightly. If he had been I wouldn't have admired—longed for him so passionately. To have visioned any outcome could have been ridiculous. As it was, a few precious moments in his presence were sufficient to make the day glow—the sun more bright, the skies over the wild autumn landscape a clearer more translucent blue.

When the prodding, pinching and pinning were over and the bustle adjusted perfectly into place Dame Jenny, at last tired herself, suggested I might like a breath of fresh air. 'There's not much to do in the kitchen,' she said, 'the baking's over, and Jan comes tomorrow to clean the floors. Take a stroll if you want to, girl. Only don't thee go wanderin' 'bout that hill. Remember, or there'll be trouble. Understand?'

I nodded, and promised I'd take the valley lane towards the village.

It was a dazzling day, speckled with frail misty air that dappled trees and undergrowth with shimmering light. The damp earth smells were redolent with the odour of fallen leaves and tumbled ripe blackberries; there was no wind, and the extreme silence—broken only by the flap of a solitary bird's wings or scuttle of

41

some small wild creature from the bushes, emphasised autumn's magic. It had been the same when I was a child—only then the salty tang of sea mingled with all the other odours of dockland—of malt, fish, and crowds swarming round newly berthed ships had filled my young nostrils nostalgically reminding me my father Pierre would appear any day, bringing some exciting gift for his Princess.

Lost briefly in reminiscences of the past I came to the curve at the base of the hill which led in one direction towards Kerrysmoor along the route I'd driven with Rupert in the chaise. I had turned the corner when the rattle of horses' hooves and wheels approached from the opposite direction. Quickly I stepped aside and stood motionless against a hedge of willow and thorn, waiting for it to pass.

As it went by a face stared at me from the window. In a shaft of pale sunlight the features were comparatively clear—hard and set, thin-lipped, with brilliant black eyes emphasised by the extreme deep-whiteness of her complexion. A regal figure, wearing something dark, either purple or black. For some reason I felt discomforted, but it was not until the carriage had passed that I realised why.

The countenance affecting me so unpleasantly was the same I had noticed watching me from the stairs on my arrival at Kerrysmoor.

She didn't like me. There had been

42

resentment, even contempt and a kind of hatred in that concentrated gaze.

Rupert's wife. Yes, I knew intuitively without doubt it was she. Well, I had done nothing to deserve it, and if possible would avoid doing so.

But I recognised for the first time there could be dangerous obstacles confronting me in my new life.

CHAPTER THREE

The day was chill when Mr Verne and I set off in the chaise for Truro and my auspicious meeting with Signor Luigi. No sunlight swept the landscape; under the grey skies, the scattered grey hamlets appeared sombre as the smoky mine stacks standing back against the moorland hills. A thin wind blew through the almost naked branches of bushes and trees. A few gulls drifted overhead, and an occasional dead leaf brushed the window as we clattered along. I drew my cloak close under my chin, and tidied a stray, straggling curl from my cheek under the frivolous headgear, feeling suddenly out of place and uncharacteristically self-conscious.

Mr Verne was so quiet. Any slight movement from him, any contact at all would have lifted my spirits, but he gave no indication at all of any pleasure in my company, and I wondered if I could have offended him in some way the day before, or if the 'Chatelaine'—that is how I now thought of his lady wife—'the Chatelaine of Kerrysmoor'—had somehow contrived to put a barrier between us. I couldn't help remembering the cold contempt of that icy stare as she passed in the carriage the previous afternoon. It was probable, I thought, that she violently disagreed with her husband sponsoring me. She might even have some knowledge of the stage, and had made up her mind already I would be a failure and the venture a waste of money.

Well, I would have to show her how wrong she was. The challenge gradually lifted depression to determination and a burst of anger. After all, I wasn't just a nobody. Pierre, my father, had taught me from an early age how to have pride in myself, and when the occasion arose behave as his Princess. Because of this I'd gathered what education was possible during my colourful 'vagabondish' days in Falmouth, learning much from listening to conversation of all types of people, and secretly mastering the art of reading in both English and French.

So I had nothing to fear from her ladyship, I told myself stubbornly, and for the rest of the journey felt better and in a more courageous mood to meet Signor Luigi.

By the time we reached Truro the skies had

slightly brightened, though no trace of sunlight caught rooftops or the imposing shape of the Cathedral. I was surprised when we left the town centre behind and travelled towards the outskirts.

'My friend owns a property that was once a small playhouse,' Rupert told me. 'It's now only used on rare occasions and for individual cultural performances. Mostly it's empty—but to Luigi it holds memories—his own dwelling is nearby—and the acoustics are good, especially for vocal requirements and rehearsing sometimes. You may find the interior somewhat gloomy and neglected, but I can assure you, you won't have time to be depressed.'

This proved to be true.

The granite building was square and bleak-looking, of no particular period, looking more like an abandoned chapel than an ex-theatre. Except for a house huddled in trees a short distance away, and a few cottages, the landscape appeared curiously without life or activity. The house I guessed was Luigi's home, and was probably more attractive from the other side because the glint of water showed through the interlaced branches of woodland, which could have been the river winding below.

'So here we are,' I heard Mr Verne saying, as the chaise came to a halt. He took my gloved hand and helped me from the vehicle, adding a

45

second later, 'You're very quiet. Nervous?'

'No,' I told him, 'well, a little perhaps. I was just thinking how deserted everything seems—' My voice trailed off vaguely.

'Oh, Luigi likes solitude, except for opera and good music.'

'Is there an organ inside?' I asked thoughtlessly.

'Good heavens, no. There might have been once of course. Before it was a theatre, in early Methodist times the place was a chapel.'

So I'd been right. 'I *thought* so.'

'Did you now?'

'Yes. I kind of felt it.'

'Well, bring your thoughts to what is important at the moment and think of how to make a good impression on my friend,' Mr Verne said almost sternly.

I could feel myself flush, resentful that he should address me like that, as though I was a child.

'I shall do my best,' I said stiffly. 'I'm not entirely an ignoramus.'

His hand involuntarily tightened on my arm.

'Calm yourself,' he said, as we mounted the few steps to the door. 'There's no need to snap. I'm more concerned for your welfare than my own. Just be your natural self and put on no airs then everything will be all right.' There was a pause before he touched the bell-pull. 'You look—quite adorable,' he added encouragingly after a hurried glance at my profile.

The compliment startled me, sending a rush of exhilaration through my veins. I raised my head proudly in anticipation of the meeting, and as the heavy bell clanged, reverberating with a hollow sound through the silence, I smoothed my gloves and then lifted my cloak a few inches so the hem was saved from dust or catching the toes of my pointed boots.

There was a rattle of a bolt being drawn, and we went in. My instant impression was of emptiness and tall narrow windows in recesses where lamps had been lighted. At the far end was a raised platform, presumably a one-time stage. The whole effect was gloomy rather than inspiring. I could imagine in the past, before the building had been a theatre, dark-clad preachers issuing dire forebodings to congregations of sombre religious converts. The singing would be of doleful psalms and hymns.

I felt suddenly trapped, with a wild instinctive desire to turn and rush out into the fresh air. Just as quickly I came to myself again. The nerve-crisis was over, and I was aware of Mr Verne presenting another shorter figure—Signor Luigi. I lifted my right hand instinctively, and as dutifully the rather portly little man raised it to his lips brushing the tips of my fingers briefly, before straightening up to his full height so the light fell directly on his face.

His brow was wide under thick crisply curling white hair; his complexion, though olive, was flushed at the high cheek bones, and this somehow added to the intense piercing quality of curiously light grey eyes under beetling brows. A carefully clipped grey beard added to an air of almost regal distinction which was emphasised by a maroon-coloured waisted velvet jacket and carefully cut black fitting trousers. He wore a white silk neckcloth. In spite of his somewhat florid appearance, there was still an aura of theatre about him, and I guessed he had a temper and could be irascible.

My deduction proved to be correct.

Following the first introductions Rupert Verne left, saying he would return in an hour to collect me.

After that my testing period—more of an interrogation, I felt—began.

First of all, under his frightening gaze, and from the platform, he put me through my scales, not once but time after time. Then I was allowed to sing one of the faraway Celtic melodies taught to me by my father. He gave no word of criticism or encouragement— simply stared, looking, I thought, more contemptuously critical than pleased.

It's difficult now to recall exactly what further endless exercises I was put through, but at last he said flatly, 'Not too bad. You have a good range. Your voice has possibilities. But ignorant—no control—no instinctive knowledge *at all* of discipline or of what the opera demands. Have you ever heard of Wagner, Miss Lebrun? Or Offenbach? Verdi?—But no. Of course not.' He shrugged. 'You are simply raw and very doubtful material.'

My temper flared.

'You must have known that,' I said hotly. 'Rupert—Mr Verne—surely told you, or I wouldn't be here. But as a matter of fact, I *have* heard of your great composers and some singers—but I can assure you I never aspired to such—such great heights. I didn't even ask to meet you. It was *him.* Rupert—' Unconsciously the Christian name slipped out. Before he could interrupt I continued. 'Obviously you have no use for me, so I'd rather you just said so, instead of scolding and deriding.'

I broke off breathlessly.

There was a pause, then the great man—or *once* great man—said, almost appeasingly, 'My dear child, you astonish me. Famous singers in the past would have been gratified to earn even a word of criticism from Arnoldo Luigi. If I thought you had no promise do you imagine I would trouble one jot about you—' He snapped his fingers. 'Eh?'

I was confused, even a little ashamed.

'I—I'm sorry. I didn't mean. I—'

'Aha!' he smiled then, a gesture with a kind

49

of mischief, even wickedness in it, '—you have a temper, temperament. That is good. No one without the flame, the longing, the glory and despair in the blood would have a chance to stir the heart and bring audiences to joy and tears. I can give you no promise, of course. But in time perhaps, with hard work and many, many scoldings from me—well, perhaps—just *perhaps*—we may, together make something of you.'

So that was the beginning.

The following week my training in voice production and stage craft commenced under the strict tuition of Arnoldo Luigi for, hopefully, a successful debut as a possible future prima donna.

Twice weekly the Vernes' chaise drove me to Truro for long sessions that were frequently tiring, leaving me chafing at what appeared to be my own inadequacies. Luigi was an irate critic, and sparse in praise, although at points when I was in a sudden too-low an ebb or on the verge of flouncing away in a temper he would unexpectedly produce a compliment and smile to restore confidence. There were also occasions when he allowed me to revert to my own choice of Celtic ballads and give full expression to the sense of romantic drama inherited from my mother. This I discovered later was not merely for my pleasure but to provide a yardstick for judging voice control—of what I'd learned so far in giving subtle but full power to my vocal range.

'Yes,' he said once, 'you have learned something, not much, but a little. In six months' time maybe—only *maybe*, you hear me?—we will give you a real test on a real stage. For that you will have to learn to move properly.'

'But—'

'Aha!' he waved a hand disparagingly, 'do not interrupt. Sometimes you show a *minimum* of grace, yes; at others you are a calf—a young cow—or a colt galloping in. *Discipline*, Miss Lebrun. Only discipline can give the essential dignity to any singer of repute. You have yet *much* to learn in every way.'

Such admonishments frequently depressed me, at other times fired my temper. Surprisingly, he was amused then, and gradually understanding developed between us.

The months passed, bringing a winter of wild gales and high seas lashing the gaunt granite coast. Apart from sessions at Truro I spent most of my time helping Dame Jenny, or attending to my duties dusting the precious treasures and figurines in the locked room. Being there was like entering another world— mostly because the girl's portrait so dominated the atmosphere. I couldn't help wondering about her—why Rupert had replied so brusquely when I'd questioned him about it. I was sure the painting meant more to him in

51

some way than that of a mere acquisition hung where it was because it fitted the place. Was the likeness of some dead relative that his wife objected to? Or was she still alive living perhaps in another country because of a family quarrel?

I brought the subject up more than once to the old lady. She dismissed my queries with a shake of the head and fierce look each time.

'I know nothing 'bout her,' she said, 'neither should you be digging and delving. Too curious you are by half 'bout things not your business. And remember what they say—"curiosity killed the cat".'

'But I'm not a cat,' I replied pertly, sensing she was withholding at least a shred of truth.

'No. Well—sometimes you do act like one,' she remarked meaningfully—'The way you go prowling of an evening sometimes t'wards Rosecarrion. I saw you yesterday, staring up the path that's forbidden you. "If she takes one step up", I said to myself, "I'll give a shout, and have to tell the master too".'

I shrugged. 'It seems so stupid. It's only a hill, an ordinary moorland hill, and the afternoon was quiet yesterday, I'd have enjoyed a walk in a different direction for a time.'

'What you enjoy and what's allowed can be two separate things,' she told me sharply. 'You should watch yourself and take care not to anger Mr Verne. You've a deal to thank him for, and be grateful. Remember that, girl.'

I did. I remembellembered all the time, and wished I had more opportunity for telling him so. But I seldom saw him. After the first visit to Truro the chaise called for me and I was driven there alone, then picked up at a certain hour and taken back to Tregonnis in the same manner unaccompanied.

The festive season approached, and Dame Jenny and I were invited up to the big house for Christmas Day. This was the one occasion in the year I was told, when servants, tenants and family joined in a dinner at night, followed by dancing in the large hall.

'Because you are being trained for life in a larger world,' the old lady said, unable to check disapproval in her voice, 'you will be allowed to eat with her ladyship and the master at midday as well. At first the idea seemed odd to me—very odd—Lady Verne is usually so particular 'bout who's allowed such intimacy. But thinking it over I saw sense in it. After months of training with the music man you should've learned certain manners. You'll have to watch yourself and show fitting modesty so Master Verne won't be ashamed of thee.'

'You can rely on me,' I said shortly. 'Will you be there too?'

Colour rose in the old bird-like face. '*Me*? There's no need to ask that. Who do you think I am, girl? An ordinary servant?'

'Of course not. I'm sorry. I shouldn't have

asked such a stupid question.'

'It's as I said—you've still a deal to learn 'bout what to say and what not. In my opinion the less you speak in the comp'ny of her ladyship the better. Then there'll be your dress to think of. The brown silk made from the material bought last time we visited Truro should be suitable, providing you wear the lace shoulder shawl to cover you decently.'

'*That* dark thing?' I exclaimed, 'but it's so drab—almost *black*—and black and brown don't go together. The yellow fringed one would look so much more attractive—and why should I wear the brown dress anyway? There's that violet velvet. I could—'

'Tut tut! hold your tongue,' Dame Jenny said sharply. 'In her ladyship's comp'ny taste counts above everything. Remember, too—' she wagged a finger in admonishment— 'you've no fame yet; just a pupil to do the master's bidding, and *I'm* responsible for your behaviour.'

'I don't remember Mr Verne saying so,' I couldn't help replying coldly.

'There's a lot you haven't heard or know anything about,' came the tart reply. 'So have done now and no more arguments, if you please.'

I let the matter drop, resigning myself to the fact I'd have to wear the brown silk to save unpleasantness, but determined to produce a few additions and alterations at the appointed

54

time.

In my own chest of clothes used in the past for my appearances at the Golden Bird I had a number of artificial flowers and lengths of braid in striking colours of the shades that were fashionable at that period—royal blue, emerald green, magenta, plum and vivid cerise. Cerise, I thought, would be striking decoration for my hair which I should wear up-coiled for the festive occasion and could be fixed at the last minute so that it would not be noticed under the hood of my cape. I would be tactful in wearing the brown gown and shawl but would arrange it so it could easily slip down after arriving at Kerrysmoor, revealing my shoulders. The effect would be attractive but not immodest. At my breast a velvet blossom would be pinned, and providing I could get down to a stitching session unknown to Dame Jenny, I'd sew stripes of cerise braid at the dress hem, with also a brightening touch to the corsage.

The effect, after I'd removed my cloak at the big house might irritate and shock the guardian of Tregonnis, even bring a glance of distaste from Lady Verne's cold face. This didn't worry me at all; the thought of making any impression—whether good or ill, only added stimulus and a mischievous sense of excitement.

Rupert, I knew, wouldn't wish me to appear drab and dull as a humble sparrow among the

Christmas throng. His eyes would be searching for me—hopefully—from the first moment of my arrival. How did I know, or guess this? Intuition, I suppose—that electrical awareness there had been between us when our eyes had first met at the Golden Bird those months ago. Although he'd not appeared at Tregonnis for some time, I couldn't believe he didn't think of me. Deep emotion which could so easily become love was not merely a visual thing, but a joy and a pain retained in the mind, and the very air of hills, sea and driven clouds sweeping the winter skies.

There was no sense of guilt in what I felt for him, however excessive and impractical the reality might be. At the moment it would have been senseless to plan. A few hours in his company had to suffice. After all, that marble-cold barrier of a wife stood between us; he had married her, she must mean something, and he was obviously disciplined and a man of principle. If he hadn't been I wouldn't have cared for him. So trying to think things out was hopeless.

There was no answer, except that I knew without any doubt at all that no man—ever—could take his place in my heart, just as I recognised that however much he tried to deny it, he felt the same. Facing the truth released certain tensions and restraint placed on me during my weeks of tuition under Signor Luigi. As Christmas drew close, I sang about the cottage, and put more and more energy into helping Dame Jenny, running up and down stairs, lifting, cleaning, dusting, only properly containing myself when I was confined, under the enigmatic gaze of the girl in the portrait, in the treasure room.

'Don't know what's got into you,' the old lady said speculatively on one occasion. 'Like lightning you are these days—a real wild one. Still, you're a help I must say, even though your voice shakes these old walls sometimes.'

'Yes,' I thought, 'I *am* wild. Wild with happiness, and just because I'm going to spend a few hours in Rupert Verne's company.'

I sighed to myself, knowing I was stupid, but revelling in my stupidity.

The day came.

Fine sleet was blown on a wind from the sea on Christmas morning when the chaise arrived to take us to Kerrysmoor.

I had been successful in hiding the flower and ribbons in my hair under the hood of the cape, and Dame Jenny was too concerned with her own fripperies of jewels—brooches, necklaces, bracelets and glittering embellishments placed at every possible angle, to take undue notice of me. However, when the time came to have my cape removed with the assistance of a servant in the hall of the great house she was at first speechless to see me standing there, shawl already half fallen, leaving my skin feeling deliciously cool and soft.

Then she said in shocked tones from almost under her breath:

'Cover theeself. 'Tisn't decent—'

One old hand came up to assist me in obeying, but she was defeated by the unexpected appearance of Rupert through a door on the left. He was elegantly attired in a dark olive green-coloured velvet suit, with a satin waistcoat and white frilled shirt. Such details registered only vaguely after the first startled impact of us seeing each other. For a second he was taken off his guard. His strange amber eyes glowed with a warmer fire—their narrow long lids widened and he actually smiled. In a daze, with my heart quickening painfully I allowed him to touch my hand, then heard him order the servant to show Dame Jenny and myself to the ladies' retiring room where my cloak was removed and hung on a peg.

The decor was pink and gold—unexpectedly bright and frivolous looking compared with the sombre hall we'd just left. Through a long mirror I adjusted the flower at my corsage, tidied my hair and saw the artificial bloom was still secure in my curls. Then I placed the lace shawl over my arm and turned to face an outraged Dame Jenny.

''Tisn' decent,' she said in a dark undertone, almost a whisper. 'Remember who you are—'

I smiled defiantly. 'That's just what I'm
58

doing. I'm sorry if it offends you.' She said something else and attempted to push the lace to my neck, but she was too short, and I was too quick for her. The next moment I was at the door of the ante-room and out again in the big hall, followed by the old lady making clucking sounds like an ancient ruffled hen.

I shall never forget the midday meal, which was taken in the great dining room; Rupert sat at the head of the table, Lady Verne at the other end. Dame Jenny and myself faced each other on either side, and I was grateful for the large bowl of holly and greenery interlaced with scarlet satin ribbon and tiny silver bells which prevented her having a direct look at me. The fare was lavish and sumptuous, including roasted pig's head, turkey, numerous entrées and Christmas pudding heavily laced with brandy sauce.

In spite of my spinning head made dizzy with wine, I was aware at brief ecstatic moments of Mr Verne's eyes on me. I think his wife must have noticed. At one point when I glanced at her, her lips were tightly set, her black eyes smouldering with dislike. I knew very well how much she resented me.

If she'd shown one gesture of welcome or friendliness, the future might have been very different, although I don't think anything in the world could have changed my feelings for Rupert. As it was, an equal cold hostility rose in me. It was clear to me that there was little warmth between her and her husband. So I put any feelings of remorse or guilt behind me, knowing that if Rupert ever needed or wanted me I would go to him, oh so willingly.

The day passed, under a veneer of goodwill, including the usual revelry, dancing and wassailing.

When the time came to leave I said a polite farewell dutifully to her ladyship, with thanks for her hospitality. She did not smile or take my hand, merely bowed her proud head, features cold and enigmatic, under the jewels winking in her black piled hair, and remarked:

'The event is a traditional one which Mr Verne chooses to retain.'

I said nothing, but must have glanced briefly at Rupert who was standing at her side. He nodded slightly, and made a point of enclosing my gloved fingers in his palm. Through the fine material I could feel his warm blood pulsing rapidly, and as the pressure momentarily increased knew everything was well between us. During the whole evening no intimate word had been said; personal contact under the severe gaze of her ladyship and watchful beady eyes of Dame Jenny, had been impossible.

But one day, sometime, I told myself, as we walked down the terrace steps to the chaise, it would be different. Awareness of the developing emotional relationship between us could not be stilled forever. Just as snowdrops and primroses pierced the cold earth in their time, so must the strength and beauty of passion come to natural flowering.

I loved him. I was still very young, but what I felt was the oldest, richest human experience in the world. Something would happen eventually that would release tension and longing, bringing natural fulfilment. It must—it was inevitable. How, and when, was impossible even to imagine; but I was impatient, and hoped it would not be too long.

The fine sleet had turned to snow as the chaise left for Tregonnis. Quite large flakes feathered the windows in a ghostly ballet of blurred movement brought to life against the swaying light of the coach's lamps. Moors, undergrowth, and stunted trees were obscured into fitful nonentity. Dame Jenny was tense and nervous, too nervous to upbraid me then for my rebellious behaviour, though I guessed she would scold me later. One claw-like old hand was clenched on her knee. The rings flashed occasionally on the ivory knuckles when a sudden beam of light caught their brilliance. In the darkness, the jolting of wheels over the cobbles and rough ground seemed accentuated—merely imagination of course, but somehow exciting—an excitement intensified by my own heightened emotions.

Rupert—Rupert! the name was magic! The meaning of his last glance at me before we left—of my hand in his, made me want to sing and cry ridiculous lovely things to the soughing wind and snow-swept sky. He must know, I thought—he might not admit the truth yet, but soon he would, because our recognition had been mutual. In spirit we already belonged.

It was only after we entered Tregonnis and made the usual nightly inspection of the treasure room that my elation faded, subduing me to normality.

The glow of the oil lamp held by Dame Jenny suddenly brought the face of the girl in the portrait into full focus. The silver-gold hair and exquisite features seemed to assume uncanny life, and I remembered, against my will, Rupert Verne's reluctance to talk of her. Doubt clouded my happiness. I tried to dispel it, but it was no use. There was a mystery somewhere involved concerning his possession of the painting—a mystery from which I was completely excluded. My mind played this way and that in search of a possible explanation until tired from the events and activities of the day, I went to bed and fell soon into a deep sleep.

When I woke it was to find the frozen weather had turned into a thaw. Grey mist hugged the landscape through which only fading drifts of white still lingered. Enchantment had gone; Dame Jenny also seemed depressed and more uncommunicative than usual. She made no attempt to chide me, as I'd expected, but went about household tasks muttering to herself on a low key. I longed for the spring, and change in the weather, and found myself looking forward to visiting Signor Luigi again early in the New Year. He had gone to Italy for a brief respite before starting once more on my tuition.

During the first few days following my jaunt to Kerrysmoor I hope desperately for a sight of Rupert, wondering if he would make a call at the cottage. But he did not. I made excuses to myself for his absence. He had matters on the estate to attend to—duty calls to make on families working at the Verne coppermine still active, Wheal Glory, or perhaps his wife was making extra demands on his attention.

Somehow, though, no contrived explanations rang true. If he'd really wanted to see me surely he could have found a means to do so. There were several horses in the stables, and her ladyship could not have kept watch on him all the time. In any case he wasn't a weakling to be ordered about by any woman. No. Search as I would I could find no plausible reason for his apparent neglect unless it was that on thinking things over he'd decided any relationship or commitment to me would be completely impracticable and therefore to be avoided at any cost.

As usual, whenever I became too elated or distressed over any situation, my capacity to keep imagination under control suffered. I was so frustrated and tormented by longing, I took every opportunity during that short period, of slipping out of the house and taking short wanders in my thickest cloak, about the countryside, and it was in such a mood that I made my way one evening round the forbidden track curving to the left and upwards towards the wild slope of Rosecarrion, leaving Dame Jenny sleeping in her rocking chair over her needlework.

Twilight would soon fall, but when I set off, except for a thin veil of rising mist hugging the high ridge, everything was comparatively clear. The area held a brooding atmosphere of primeval menace, as though something of ancient history still lingered as guardian of the past. A narrow path wound intricately between furze and great boulders entangled by bramble and spiky gorse. In spite of my boots I kept my eyes alert for any snake-like shape slithering from a stone or root of stunted tree. Although the air was so still, hidden life seemed everywhere. I was fascinated—a little keyed-up and on edge, but through curiosity impelled to go on.

Not realising I had climbed quite so far, I paused a quarter of the way up the hill, and searched the land in every direction. Daylight had almost faded leaving a queer greenish glow behind the misted summit. It was when I turned to the west that I saw with surprise the ribbon of lane below cutting abruptly inwards above and around a gully filled by a gently lapping tide. I hadn't known how near the coast the path had led me. At times in rough weather the locality would be dangerous—a fall over the high cliffs only too easy for the unwary. Was that why Rupert had forbidden me to go that way?

For some moments I stood motionless watching, and as a frail belt of cloud lifted there was movement where the slope of land met sky; a man's shape emerged from the tumbled ruins of what could once have been the relics of a cottage or old mine workings, and made his way round a further bend away from me, until he was lost to sight. His figure had been humped at a curious angle, and I wondered if he'd been carrying something; a poacher perhaps?

If I'd not been away from Tregonnis for so long or afraid that Dame Jenny might already be angrily waiting for me I'd have cut round to the right to find out where the path led. There were so many bewildering tracks winding from the point where I was standing. One leading directly down towards the creek was wider and appeared to have been well-trodden recently. It was all very bewildering; a torn piece of material—probably from a neckscarf or kerchief hung on a jagged briar nearby. So *someone* had walked or ridden that area not long ago. Tinkers, or gypsies?

I was still ruminating when a bird rose screeching from behind a boulder on my left. I turned my head, then glanced upwards at the dark winged shape soaring to the sky. At that very moment a shaft of light zig-zagged down the hill, through the quickly fading half light, wavered, and circled round the moor, missing my form by only a few feet.

Just as suddenly as it had appeared, the light swung upwards and disappeared, but not before my startled eyes had recognised in a brief lifting of cloud, the stark shapes of the Three Maidens outlined for an instance on the horizon. Even seen at a different angle from my first glimpse of them, the gaunt stones held the same quality of menace and impending doom. Drawing my cloak close I turned quickly and made my way towards the valley. Unfortunately I chose the wrong path and had to make a detour guided only by the distant outline of the mine, Wheal Glory, against the moor.

By the time I reached the cottage it was quite dark. The old lady was standing at the gate huddled into her shawl with a lantern in one hand.

'You've had me frightened,' she exclaimed, almost in a high-pitched scream. 'Where've'ee been? The Master called earlier, soon after thee'd gone out. There came a rap on th' door. I was dozin' and it set my heart all of a flutter. But that wasn't the point. The point was you should say when you're taking off for a stroll, and tell me where. He didn't like it when I couldn't say, and rode off very put out—' She broke off breathlessly.

'I'm sorry,' I said lamely, and I was. Not only on account of Dame Jenny's distress, but because I'd missed Rupert.

I wondered what he wanted me for.

The next day I knew.

He'd heard from Signor Luigi that he was returning earlier than expected from Italy, having learned of an opportunity to launch me as Lucy Lockett in John Gay's *Beggars' Opera* scheduled to open at an Exeter theatre in three weeks' time. The actress Linda Dewhurst who had rehearsed for the role had been suddenly taken ill which had left the part open for anyone with the looks, and capacity to learn quickly, who also possessed the necessary vocal qualities and acting ability. There was no understudy, owing to the young lady's having been dismissed two days previously through a serious quarrel with the manager.

Hence my chance.

All this was explained to me the next morning by Rupert seated opposite to me in the front parlour of Tregonnis. 'You're very lucky,' he said. 'If Signor Luigi had not been an intimate friend of Frederick Allen and able to contact him so quickly some other actress might have been found. As it is—' He smiled and for a few seconds the years fell away. His whole face changed, became younger, warm with pride, affection, and ambition for me. Then he continued more seriously, 'Aren't you

67

pleased? Surely it's what you wanted—to appear on a real stage before an audience fully qualified to appreciate your voice and—you?'

In a whirl of conflicting emotions—delight, excitement, mingled with doubt, apprehension and awe, I answered, 'Oh, yes. Of course. But—' I swallowed painfully '—my voice isn't properly trained yet. After my last lesson Signor Luigi told me I bellowed like a barmaid, and moved like a—like a horse or something.' I shook my head 'I don't think I'd be right for this—this Lucy person *really*.'

'*You* may not think so,' I heard Rupert remarking, quite unperturbed, 'but I've complete faith in my friend's judgement. If he's willing to back you I'm sure I am. As for his criticism—' he shrugged, displaying the palms of both hands in a dismissive gesture '—Luigi wouldn't waste one breath on you if he didn't recognise your talent. He can be more than forthright—even offensive to some when he feels like it—but only when he considers the material is worthwhile. It's his way of getting the best out of a pupil.'

'A rather odd way,' I remarked pertly. 'Not usual, surely?'

'But then neither are you.'

He got up, came towards me, and drew me to my feet. I was wearing a violet-coloured daydress I remember, made by my own hand with the help of the old lady, from a piece of material Pierre had brought me on his last visit

68

to Falmouth, and which I'd kept hoarded away in my small chest with a few other treasures. It had a white lace collar and cuffs, and fell in soft folds, drawn gently to the back from a nipped-in waist. Dame Jenny had told me when I came downstairs that day that it was too elegant for normal use. I had agreed with her and promised to change as soon as possible into something more suitable.

I was pleased now that I hadn't. Those passionate enigmatic eyes of the man who so desperately fascinated me, were for once alight in obvious fiery admiration. His hands released mine suddenly, and were on my shoulders. Automatically I raised my head. A few curls fell from their combs and brushed my neck softly.

'You're very—beautiful, Josephine,' he said in low, slightly husky tones. 'And your eyes— you're a subtle creature to wear blue—'

'Violet,' I corrected him.

'Violet, then. Dammit what does it matter? You know well enough how lovely you are—'

Through my wild excitement a thought struck me. On impulse I spoke. 'Am I? Am I *really?* As lovely as—as that girl in the painting? The one hanging in the treasure room?'

I shouldn't have said it. It was a grave mistake, and in a moment I knew. He drew away from me abruptly. His gaze was hard when he faced me again. Dull with disappointment, because I'd known he'd been about to kiss me, furious with myself for the stupid blunder, I heard him remark in remote tones, 'Comparisons are odious. If I pay a compliment it should be taken for that and no more. I'm afraid you have still a few things to learn about tact and etiquette.'

'Of course I have,' I said hotly. 'I'm not gently bred like your lady wife, and—'

'Leave my wife out of it, if you please,' he said curtly, 'and curb that wild temper of yours. Do you understand?'

'Certainly,' I retorted, feeling the warm blood rush to my cheeks. 'In future I'll curtsey to you when you address me, if you choose, and remember to say "sir" on every occasion we speak.'

His mood suddenly changed. He laughed. 'You'll make an admirable Lucy Lockett, I'm sure. So enough of your moods, Miss Lebrun. On Thursday you'll be driven to Truro. I shall accompany you, and we'll see what arrangement Signor Luigi intends to make regarding the performance.'

'He may not think I'm good enough when he hears me singing again,' I pointed out, 'and if I move like a horse—'

'You won't,' he stated firmly. 'You'll be your natural graceful self with your voice and fiery tongue under equal control.'

'And if I don't wish to appear at Exeter?' I persisted stubbornly.

70

He paused before saying significantly, 'I think you will, because *I* wish it.'

And in that he was right.

The interview ended shortly after arrangements for the following Thursday had been concluded. At the door Rupert took my hand briefly and raised it to his lips—a polite gentlemanly gesture of farewell, no more. It was as though he was determined to erase any former show of sentiment, subduing passion under a mask of wellbred formality. I waited hopefully for his eyes once more to rest on mine, but they did not.

Dame Jenny appeared in the hall, holding out his stove hat and cane. He took them murmuring a quiet thank you. The last I saw of him that day was his caped figure walking smartly down the path to the lane where the chaise waited.

Seconds later he had gone.

CHAPTER FOUR

On the evening before my visit to Signor Luigi, I received a note from Rupert delivered by a Kerrysmoor servant, saying that he would not after all be able to accompany me to Truro owing to an unexpected matter of business arising. He apologised, but sent his best wishes, adding that he was sure everything would go

71

well, that 'the maestro' would confirm my suitability to play the role of Lucy, and that when next we met I should have good news for him. The brief epistle ended on a formal note— 'Yours with every encouragement, Rupert Verne.'

I stared blankly at the sheet for some moments, heavy with disappointment. What possible business could he have, I thought unreasonably, that should have to be dealt with just at the time I was depending on him for support? And why couldn't he have fixed whatever it was at another hour or day? I'd looked forward so much to sitting beside him in the chaise with no one to disturb our proximity, imagined the touch of his hand on mine, savoured in advance the exciting closeness of his body, the pressure of an arm as the coach jolted or lurched over a rough piece of roadway.

The warmth of his breath would mingle with mine—his lips brush my cheek; and when in delight and confusion I looked up into those strange golden eyes they would be hot with desire, and I would be close against him, my whole body alight with flowering love. However short the contact, he'd recognise the futility of denial. What happened in the future would be of his choice, which I would abide by, because he was the man, and considerably older than I. I was in no position to make plans. All I could do was to submit, given the chance.

The chance?

But apparently either other things came first, or he was not prepared to endanger one iota of his status and good name in society.

Utterly depressed I tore the piece of paper into shreds and threw them into the parlour fire, watching them gradually curl, blaze, then disintegrate into smoke.

After a time I forced myself to a more philosophical mood. Whether I was successful or not in persuading Signor Luigi that I was sufficiently competent for the role in *The Beggar's Opera* I was bound to come face to face with Rupert on some future occasion. So the important thing was to be a success, and make him proud of me.

Before retiring that evening I tried out my voice in my bedroom, choosing a song that had been one of my mother's favourites. There was no hoarseness or flaw in my vocal chords, no quiver of hesitancy or lack of control. I stood at the window giving full range to any talent I possessed, singing—singing—and realising at the same time how much I had learned under the strict tuition of the fierce little Italian.

When it was over I waited motionless for a short time, with my eyes fixed on the moonlit landscape. The window faced from the side of Tregonnis, overlooking Rosecarrion and part of the area where I'd wandered before Christmas. There was a wind, and the scene was one of purple and blue shadows lit by fleeting splashes of gold. The Three Maidens were nowhere in view, being cut off to the left, but if I strained my head and gazed to the other side a glimmer of sea could be glimpsed in the far distance.

I was staring in that direction when I saw something else—something not shadow or stunted tree waving in the wind—a crouched moving shape that I took at first to be that of some large animal on night prowl. Then as the form partly disintegrated, or rather split up, I realised it was a group. Small dots of figures took an upward course towards what I imagined must be the ruined building—cottage or mineworks—that I'd seen on my forbidden exploration weeks before.

In the constantly changing vista of light and sudden shadow it was difficult to be sure or even guess what they were about. Poachers probably I told myself, as I had before, or could they be fishermen plodding to their homes after a hard day at sea? Perhaps the track provided a short cut to outlying cottages over the ridge of moor.

Whatever the explanation, I had an uneasy feeling that something strange was going on, and determined to question Dame Jenny about it in the morning.

When daylight came, however, I was far too busy and excited to bother. I had only a light breakfast, and at eight o'clock as arranged the chaise arrived to take me to Truro. I wore my best attire and most frivolous headgear, and had even applied a touch of rose lipsalve to my mouth, purloined wickedly in a hasty moment from a tiny jar that Dame Jenny had left carelessly on a mantelshelf. My cheeks were already over-bright from excitement and for this I used a film of rice powder. The result gave me confidence and an elated sense of sophistication. There was a hint of suspicion in the old lady's eyes as she bid me farewell, with affection, yet admonishment as well in her voice.

'Good luck, child,' she said, 'and remember to be modest and careful how ye do address the great music-man. Talent you must have, or the master wouldn' be doin' all this for thee. But good manners count always, remember that.'

I glanced back, smiling at her over my shoulder. 'I'll do my best,' I said, and meant it.

The day was fine, and pale winter sunlight spread its gold over the city, and all around giving added enchantment to the occasion which wasn't however entirely without trepidation on my part. But I needn't have worried.

Signor Luigi, instead of appearing fierce and over-critical that day as he usually was, acted in an entirely different manner, being quite flattering and warm in encouragement following my tryout of Lucy Lockett's first ditty in the opera.

75

'That is good,' he said. 'There are points here and there needing strict attention, and you still have much to study of stagecraft. We have three weeks of intensive training before us, during which, in your spare time you must learn—*learn*, until words come automatically without thought. I shall scold you maybe sometimes, perhaps very often, and you must expect my friend, the producer, will do more of it during the two days in Exeter before the opening performance. Well?' He cocked his head sideways like an inquisitive robin, 'do you wish to become Lucy Lockett for a time, Miss Josephine? And if so—can you promise solemnly to obey instructions without argument or show of your fiery temper? It is a great chance you have before you. Do not forget it.'

I agreed with alacrity. 'Oh yes—yes. If you think I'm good enough, of *course*—' I cried.

'I do not think you are yet good,' he told me with a whimsical smile. 'But you have grace and talent. See that you apply both to the best of your ability and I'm sure no one will have cause to complain.'

So it was that I returned to Tregonnis that evening able to tell Dame Jenny of my success, wishing at the same time that Rupert was there to hear the news.

During the following weeks most of my time was spent in Truro. It was a period of conflicting moods—of expectancy, exhilaration, optimism and disappointments combined with physical exertion that left me too tired at the end of each day to brood on other matters. Luigi, anxious that I should not *over*-strain my voice, included hours of concentrated dramatic tuition that occasionally so irritated and frustrated me, I could have screamed. However, I miraculously managed to keep any nervous reaction under control—outwardly, though Dame Jenny commented frequently that I was touchy and on edge at Tregonnis.

'I must say you do speak over-sharp to me these days,' she commented once. 'I hope when the master calls you'll remember to be more polite.'

'I don't think the master's much interested in me or what I'm doing,' I replied shortly, and I had really begun to believe this was true, since he'd looked in at the cottage only once during the first fortnight of rehearsing, and had then appeared remote and withdrawn as though he had other more important affairs on his mind.

'That's a wicked thing to say,' the old lady retorted irately, "specially when he's paying a little fortune to get you where you want to be.'

'I didn't expect or ask him to launch me,' I replied, 'or for his money either. This *Beggar's Opera* business and the lessons with Signor Luigi were forced on me—in a way.'

'Nonsense.' The one word came out explosively, like a pistol shot. 'I do recall very well the day at Christmas when you flaunted yourself before his eyes with your shoulders bare, and that wicked gypsy look in your eyes. Oh you were all out to make an impression, girl, so no trying to pull the wool over my eyes.'

I flushed, bit my lip, and was silent. It was true, I *had* wished Rupert to notice me, and contrived to make myself as spectacular as possible. And I had not entirely failed; the memory of his warm glances on me and the mutual interest between us—the understanding that had so fiercely flamed for those few revealing moments, returned painfully, stirring me with sudden longing.

When I didn't speak, Dame Jenny said in more conciliatory tones, 'Now, now! There's no need to be cast down. Just take heed of a bit of advice, that's all, and remember what the master've told you; if what you said was true, get as much fresh air in your spare time to relax thee and keep the breath sweet in your lungs. I won't be bothering asking so much where you've been so long as you're back to time. "Don't chain her too hard," Mr Verne said the other afternoon when he was passing, "she's a free spirit," he said, "let her roam a bit, t'will do her no harm."'

"I didn't know he'd called, you didn't tell me.'

'I don't report on every small happening of the day, girl. 'Tisn't my duty to do so. I'm only tellin' thee now for your own encouragement.

You were a bit later back from Truro than usual or you'd have seen him for thyself.'

I recalled that on one occasion the signor had pressed me into staying at rehearsal for an extra half an hour to get my words better perfected. What a nuisance, I thought, that Rupert had chosen the very time to visit Tregonnis.

Still, I was slightly uplifted by the knowledge he'd taken the trouble to call at all, and decided his advice to Dame Jenny was right. I needed fresh air and exercise.

It was a fine afternoon. Clouds of the morning had cleared, leaving the countryside splashed with pale golden sunshine. Quite soon it would start to sink lower in the sky, sending long shadows snaking down the moors, but if I started immediately—it was only four o'clock—I would have almost an hour for an enjoyable stroll.

So I set off wearing boots and a loose grey cloak to cover my gown, taking the lane round the base of Rosecarrion. I didn't venture to climb the hill—the air was sweet enough in the valley, heady with the scents of early spring, and I had an urge to follow the roadway in the direction of the sea where the moor cut so sharply and surprisingly inwards to the gully. With my eyes averted from glancing upwards at the Three Maidens sloping slightly sideways at a peculiar angle, their menace for me had abated a little during the hectic period of

79

intense rehearsals, and when a fleeting memory of them *had* occurred I'd told myself reasoningly that their unpleasant impact had only lingered because the rigid starkness of the ancient stones reminded me in a childish way of the rigid coldness of Rupert's lady wife.

It was pleasant walking. As I neared the gully—it was really a very narrow creek—the smell of brine mingled with that of heather, damp sweet earth, and all the other odours of thrusting young life and herbage. The narrow river on the opposite side of the lane had curved abruptly in another direction, away from the coast, but the gaunt cliffs loomed precipitously close to the road, and the shadowed cut in the lane appeared as though giants' teeth had taken a savage bite leaving a cruel void of darkness and death for the unwary.

I paused, held by the wild fascination of the scene. It was then that I glimpsed movement, and after a moment's astonishment was able to distinguish close against the far side of the inlet a vessel at anchor. Details or name of the ship were impossible to discern. In the slowly fading light and shadows of overhanging cliffs boat and rocks were almost blended into one.

At first I'd thought I could be mistaken, but I wasn't. When I moved forward a human shape appeared on deck, followed by another. Their appearance was only brief. In a few seconds they'd disappeared—moved below. But my heart jerked. In that fleeting space of time something about the first figure had been curiously familiar—the build and way of moving in the caped coat—his bold erect stance and sudden manner of turning and striding away bore an uncanny resemblance to Rupert. I was puzzled; what could Rupert Verne be doing at such at hour aboard a strange vessel in such an unlikely, dangerous, and remote harbour?

I managed presently to convince myself I'd been wrong, and had concocted unconsciously an image of the man who was always so deep in my mind. Even then doubts lingered. I waited a little longer wondering if the forms would return. But they did not. A single dot of light flickered for a moment then disappeared. All was dark. The sky, too, had quickly faded, merging the horizon of sea and land into one.

Hoping Dame Jenny would be unaware of my over-long absence from the house, I turned and took the thread of curving lane as quickly as possible back to Tregonnis.

*　　*　　*

The day for travelling to Exeter for the opening performance at the Regal Opera House at last arrived. I was given a sleeping potion the evening before to enable me to face the journey calmly, in the company of Mr Verne and his lady wife, who, unfortunately for me, insisted

81

upon being present herself at my debut. We journeyed by luxury four horse omnibus from Truro to Plymouth, where we stayed the night. In the morning we set off by rail for Exeter, arriving at the city by four-thirty in the afternoon. Signor Luigi accompanied us for which I was grateful. He had a stabilising influence on my growing excitement and nervous tension, and although being quite tired conversation was intermittent, his presence kept me less conscious of Lady Verne's cold stare than otherwise I would have been.

She was looking quite regal in a plain-coloured wild crimson silk gown, under a silver grey paletot with a shoulder cape. Bands of velvet braid and plum covered buttons completed an elegant effect, and her bonnet of the same shades was worn at a fashionable angle, revealing glossy glimpses of shining black hair in contrast to the extreme magnolia pallor of her finely set features.

I wore a new cape which her ladyship had insisted on choosing herself. It was of good quality, but as usual, brown, and rather severe, giving no glamour to my looks. My bonnet-hat, too, was ordinary. However, I contrived to add a length of green ribbon and a spray of shining leaves to brighten the effect, and from the look on my lady's face when she noticed, I knew I'd succeeded in my objective.

When I think back now on the next few days,

no words can express the conflict of emotions—confusion, excitement, and daze of events following one upon the other at such speed my head still whirls. It was like living in a dream. I was both bewildered and exhilarated by the luxury of the hotel overlooking gardens, the delicious meals, impeccable service, the rose and gold furnishings, rich carpeting and soundless approach of servants and footmen to fulfil our slightest wish. My bedroom was huge, ornately furnished with an elegance I'd imagined existed only for royalty or in fairy tales. If I had not been so physically tired I wouldn't have slept at all that night. But the great bed was so soft and comfortable, I drifted almost at once into dreamless slumber, waking up only when a maid servant arrived with morning tea.

After breakfast I was taken on a shopping expedition to equip me more suitably to meet the manager in the afternoon at the theatre. He was a tall, thin man with an eagle gaze and brusque manner. He wore an eye-glass and seldom stood still, but walked to and fro unsmilingly, taking, I thought, only cursory glances at me. He made me sing a scale, move, turn, bow and curtsey, all the time frowning a little, then nodding. Eventually he said:

'All right, all right. That's enough. I hope you know your words. There'll be a rehearsal in half an hour; Elise—' He turned his head towards the wings from where a small woman in black silk appeared as though she'd been waiting for a cue '—Take Miss—Miss—?' He glanced at me enquiringly.

'Lebrun. Josephine Lebrun,' Signor Luigi interposed for me.

'Take Miss Lebrun to the dressing room,' the manager continued, 'and see she's attired appropriately as Lucy.' He scrutinised me closely then added, 'Green I think. The emerald green. Red is more usual for the role but would be atrocious with this girl's colouring.'

Trying not to feel mildly squashed, I did as I was bid and followed the little woman to the back of the stage, and along a maze of narrow dark passages and doors. The room we entered was small and stuffy, smelling mustily of dust, perspiration and makeup. There were several mirrors and tables placed about, and obviously I was not to be the only occupant. I had thought such places—anything to do with the stage—would be glamorous. But there was no glamour here, although gowns of different shades hung from pegs and an open wardrobe, and an array of gaudy glittering jewellery lay displayed giving an impression of brightness. Various pots of paint and cream cluttered shelves, and a young woman with brassy yellow hair was already seated at a dressing table cleaning her face with a cloth.

'Miss Annette Gold,' I was told by the dresser, 'she is the star of the production. A

84

well-known actress—you must have heard of her—she plays Polly Peachum. It's a privilege for you to have a role opposite to her. If it hadn't been for—' she broke off suddenly, continuing after taking a deep breath, '—but never mind. We can only hope that you come up to scratch. It's always a chancy business taking on an unknown player. Had any experience at all, have you?'

'Oh yes, some,' I answered not feeling it was a lie when I recollected the long arduous hours spent with Signor Luigi at Truro, and also my performances at the Golden Bird.

'Hm! that's as well.'

She bustled around telling me to disrobe as time was short for all to be punctual for the rehearsal. Clad only in bodice and pantalettes, I was then directed to sit on a stool to be pummelled, rubbed and slapped about the face by the make-up artist, until I was considered in adequate shape for being painted and powdered—garishly I thought—for the role of Lucy. When I saw myself through the mirror I was not only astonished but dismayed. The voluptuous-looking highly-coloured creature was a travesty of my real self—looking more like a successful prostitute from Dockland than Pierre's cherished 'princess'.

'But that can't be *me*!' I gasped.

'You're not supposed to be "you". You're Lucy Lockett,' came the quick reply.

'But my lips—so bright! And my *eyes*!'

85

'If you'd any knowledge of the stage, which you said you had, you'd know that under the lights and to the audience you'll look quite different. And Lucy, remember, is a bold character. Now just keep calm and we'll see if the dress is right.'

Whether right or wrong the brilliant emerald-green velvet was certainly spectacular, and with a little swift taking-in at the waist fitted perfectly. My dismay gave place to incredulity, holding a certain mischievous pleasure, when at last, with my dark curls pulled back in a sophisticated style, one lock left to fall on a bare shoulder, I surveyed my full length reflection through a long glass. I was trembling a little, and gasping from excitement. The bodice was cut so low at the bosom, the nipples of my breasts almost showed. I pulled one side of the material up—or tried to. It was no use. There was a short laugh from somewhere behind me. I turned. Polly Peachum was standing there looking more attractive than I'd expected in a pink period gown, with a white apron and pretty white mob-cap.

'Got the jitters, have you?' she asked. 'Nerves. Well, it's natural. I've been hearing things.'

'What things?'

'How it's your first real part in opera. Raw beginner, aren't you? But don't you fret. You'll do all right. Willie will be along presently. He'll tell you.'

'Who's Willie?'

'Willie Spark, stage manager and assistant director; an acquaintance of that fine lady something or other who brought you along—'

'Of Lady *Verne*?'

'Yes, that's it. Oh, I don't mean they're *friends* or anything like that, they just met once or twice in the past, when she was in London. Willie's quite a character—a bit talkative when he's under the influence—you know—' she gave an imitation of lifting a glass to her lips '—but comes of a good family, the reprobate, so to speak. A charmer though. Could charm the hind legs off a horse so to speak. Clever in his way.'

When I met him, during a break in the rehearsal, I agreed. He was quick and deft at organising scenic effects in the least possible time, and had as well a soothing effect on the players, never scolding or becoming irate; his good looks and amiable disposition in fact had the whole cast comparatively cheerful, and only too willing to follow his suggestions. Obviously he was a bit of a dandy—his attire was colourful, and reminiscent of an earlier decade—artistic rather than fashionable, including a gold velvet waistcoat, and silk cravat with a yellow bow-tie. I got little praise for my performance from the producer, but when the tiring session of the rehearsal was over, Willie—everyone called him that—

87

congratulated me. 'You will make a most picturesque Lucy,' he said, 'and the range of your voice was most remarkable.'

Such compliments raised my spirits, and later, at the hotel I was able to face Rupert and his icy wife with confidence, even a hint of pride. I hadn't expected to have 'to run through the play' again—the producer's words—on Sunday. Lady Verne openly disapproved, and I knew if Dame Jenny had known, so would she. But it was held in the afternoon, following morning service at Exeter Cathedral where her ladyship had appeared extremely smart and devout in black silk relieved by a touch of crimson. I'd been forced once more to wear my sober brown cape. I'd hoped desperately that there would be a chance for Rupert to show me some of the sights, but there was no time, and even if there had been I guessed her odious ladyship would have insisted on accompanying us. On the Monday morning a further rehearsal followed, and in the afternoon I was ordered to rest before the great occasion of the opening night at the theatre.

Oh, how highly-wrought and on edge I felt. So much depended on the result of this debut. Waiting in the wings for my first appearance was sheer torture. My spine was rigid, alternate waves of icy cold and heat flooded me. At one moment my heart raced so wildly I thought I'd faint. But Willie, mercifully, sensing the ordeal, came to my aid speedily, smiling, and with a small glass containing a potion of clear liquid. In a moment, when no-one could observe me, he handed it to me, whispering, 'Drink that up, darling, it will revive and steady you. And have no fear. Without nerves you'd be no actress. You'll be splendid—' he withdrew quickly, and automatically I obeyed and swallowed the potion.

For minutes afterwards I felt comforted and calm, eager, in fact, to make my entrance. The stimulant, combined with the knowledge that I looked well in the striking green velvet, and that Rupert had the best seat in the dress circle to watch, filled me with sudden overpowering joy. My head felt light, even my legs were a little unsteady, but I knew my voice was in good form. I would be a successful rival to Polly Peachum. Rupert would be proud of me—I would become a great singer, just for him.

At last my cue came.

Lifting my head I swept—almost tottering—on to the stage. The lights at first bewildered me, then, at a sign from the stage manager, as the accompaniment struck up, I opened my mouth for the first full-throated notes to emerge.

What exactly happened next I can't clearly recall—only that for a dreadful few seconds no sound came. My throat felt dry, parched. I took a deep breath and a harsh croak shattered the air. I paused and tried again. It was useless, terrifying. What had happened? Where had my voice gone? I couldn't sing. From shocked astonishment the audience gave vent to low 'boos' and muffled laughter that quickly changed to guffaws of derision. Rude comments were shouted as I struggled for composure, to refrain from swooning. My last conscious memory was of the curtain rattling down and white masks of faces crowding round as I was pulled and half-carried from the stage to the dressing room.

Then mercifully oblivion claimed me, and when I came to myself I was in a cab being taken back to the hotel, sick, faint, a failure, and wishing I could die.

CHAPTER FIVE

For two days following the terrible episode leading to the disgrace and failure of what should have been my successful debut as a singer and actress, a depressing silence lay like a pall over Tregonnis. Dame Jenny said little, but I sensed she was not unsympathetic.

'Never mind,' she said. 'Showing off to a lot of folk isn't all that important. To my mind 'tis a far more honourable accomplishment knowing how to bake a good cake or stitch a tidy sampler. Cheer up, my maid. Thee'll discover all in good time that it was for the best. Life has a cunning pattern to it that's not always seen till later when it's clear as daylight.'

'I failed,' I answered. 'I was just no good, and Mr Verne there!—I'll never forget, *never*. And I can't *understand*. I hadn't my voice at all—my throat was dry, and when I opened my mouth it was as though all breath went, and—and my head ached so. I couldn't even *see* properly. There must have been a reason. But what?—*What?*'

'Now, now, don't work thyself into a tizzy,' the old lady remarked calmly. 'Probably it was nerves brought on a turn. Anyway the doctor will find out when he calls.'

'The doctor?'

'Her ladyship's specialist. I had word brought by Jan, farmer Carne's boy, about an hour ago, that he'd be calling this morning to give an examination.'

'On *me*?'

Dame Jenny nodded. 'And quite right, too.'

I was suddenly suspicious, and for no logical reason I suppose, but anything to do with Lady Verne was hateful to me.

'Did she write it?'

'No, the Master. I have it here. You can read it if you like.'

She went to her own small desk and handed me an envelope. I took the piece of paper out, and read:

Just a word, ma'am, to say that Doctor Zane, my lady wife's medical adviser, will be calling this morning about twelve o'clock to make certain Miss Lebrun has fully recovered from her collapse and that she is suffering no signs of serious illness. His professional opinion will then be conveyed to me, and we will be in a position to decide her future.

Yours faithfully,
Rupert Verne.

I handed the note back to her.

'I see. Thank you.'

So formal, so cold; so detached as though I was some embarrassing commodity or horse from the stables, to be priced and sold, if necessary, to a convenient bidder.

A horse! I remembered vividly the occasion on which Signor Luigi had likened my movements to one of the species. Perhaps it was true, I thought, reviewing my status disparagingly. Perhaps the fire in Rupert's eyes for me had kindled merely because I'd appeared a worthwhile investment. If so, how shamefully I had been deceived.

Involuntarily the nails of both hands dug hard into my clenched palms.

'So we shall have to abide by the doctor's verdict,' I heard Dame Jenny saying fatuously. 'And if—'

'I don't think the doctor will find anything

wrong with my health,' I interrupted sharply. 'And whether he does or not, I'm quite capable of deciding my own future.'

'Maybe. But you've got to remember all the Master's done for thee, which leaves you indebted to him, surely?'

'I shall be able to repay anything that's been spent on me,' I said, lifting my head proudly. 'I lived quite profitably before, and can do so again, if necessary.'

'Hoity-toity! Singing in cheap inns and houses of ill-fame do 'ee mean? An' suppose you do suffer another fit like the one at Exeter?'

'It wasn't a fit. It was—'

I broke off because I had no explanation to give, unless—I suddenly stiffened. My spine went rigid and my senses froze as I recalled the draught given to me by Willie, who had not only been stage manager at the theatre, but also an acquaintance of Lady Verne. Why had the connection not occurred to me before? Or could it have been coincidence? Whatever the answer I had no way of proving it. Neither would the doctor be of any use. I felt intuitively that he would do his best to prove me an unreliable character given to fits of hysteria which would make me therefore quite unsuitable for a serious stage career. Yes, the doctor was a friend of her ladyship and this was exactly what she would wish.

Perhaps I was being mean in attributing such unethical conduct to a man I'd never met; but half an hour later, when he walked into the parlour my instinctive suspicions were intensified.

He was a small portly figure, over-elegantly dressed for a professional man, with a smooth tongue, obsequious manners, and a way of smiling with his lips but not his eyes, that discomforted me.

In Dame Jenny's presence he made me unbutton my bodice, then with odious plump fingers started tapping here and there, lingering sensuously for a second or two about my breasts where I clutched my camisole tightly above the nipples.

At last, becoming irritated with such an unobliging patient, he released me, put his stethoscope away, and remarked in bored booming tones, 'Nothing I can find wrong with you at all—*physically*. That you should lose your voice and go into a swoon on such an important occasion denotes a certain nervous instability, no more. I will inform your master and her ladyship that there is no need for concern. That is all then, thank you!'

He gave a little bow, collected his bag, and with the old lady fluttering before him to open the door, left.

When she returned I remarked derisively, 'I *thought* so.'

'What do you mean, girl?'

'That he'd try to make me out a half-wit and hysteric,' I answered bluntly. 'Being Lady

94

Verne's doctor, he *would*.'

'Now that's not at all a nice thing to say,' the old lady said, pursing her lips. 'It just shows you're not yourself. Her ladyship and the Master've done all they could to bring you fame and riches. But you weren't bred for it, girl, and—'

'What do you mean *bred* for it?' I flashed, before she could finish. 'My breeding—if you *must* use such an obnoxious word, is as good as any in the land. My mother was beautiful, of a respectable Welsh family, and my father was a fine Breton seaman. He died in a wreck, bringing food to this country, and both my parents had a love of music. He taught me early how to sing and to learn good language. They weren't rich or anything, but what does that matter? Money's nothing without happiness or talent. And they loved each other. *Really* loved.'

I broke off breathlessly, feeling suddenly so low and depressed I could have broken into sobs. But I didn't. What point was there in crying when the old lady would merely have taken it as proof of the doctor's opinion that I was indeed nervously unstable, and that my terrible stage debut had been the result of a fit of hysterics? It was important I controlled myself, giving a show of pride, whatever doubts her ladyship and Doctor Zane contrived to instill into Rupert's mind.

After a short pause I heard Dame Jenny say

95

placatingly, 'No one suggested anything against your folk. You're fancying things, girl. Perhaps it's natural, after what you've been through. I was just pointing out to thee, that persons of high standing like the master and his lady wife are on a different level from us humbler kind, which you'd do well to remember.'

'Social levels mean nothing to me,' I stated, a little rudely perhaps.

'No. You've made that clear,' she said sharply. 'But it will be to the benefit of both of us if you behave in a proper manner when Master Verne calls.'

'He may not call at all.'

'Oh yes, indeed he will,' came the reply. 'Tomorrow sometime, after he's had the doctor's report.'

And he did.

Against Dame Jenny's specific instructions I wore the violet velvet, ignoring her fumings, which at one point almost rose to high-pitched screaming. She'd probably also noticed I'd applied a little lip salve which gave me confidence.

'I told thee 'twasn't seemly for the occasion,' she cried, thrusting her old chin forward aggressively. 'Why you've got to be so stubborn an' headstrong I don't know. Shameless, you are. *Shameful*. There's a devil in 'ee an' that's f'r sure. Just when it's right to show a little modesty you come downstairs lookin' like a strumpet from a bad-house—'

I strolled over to the mirror, lifted my chin, and loosened a stray dark curl from the lilac ribbons that held it, so it fell against one cheek softly. Then I shrugged, appearing more nonchalant that I felt.

'As you think of me in that way surely it's correct to be obvious.'

'And now, on top of it all—impudence,' she muttered raspingly.

'Perhaps,' I agreed. 'If so I've nothing to lose. Let Master Verne see me as *you* do, a strumpet, then maybe you'll be rid of me sooner than you expected.'

It was a cruel statement to make because I knew in many ways I was of great help to the old lady, and that she'd miss me sorely. But tart words just then seemed the only possible way to ease my tension during the waiting period for Rupert Verne's arrival.

He came in the afternoon looking tired and a little worried, but so incredibly handsome my heart lurched in the old familiar way, but more intensely, more longingly, mingled with a dread feeling of hopelessness.

He dismissed Dame Jenny tactfully, bade me sit down, then walked to the window, staring towards the garden for a few seconds before turning again to me.

'I hope you've recovered,' he said before easing himself against the table, half sitting, half standing. 'I had the doctor's report yesterday evening.'

'Oh yes,' I murmured over-casually. 'I can guess what it was.'

'Indeed?' his voice was sceptical, but his eyes were so intent on my face I turned my gaze away, trying to quell the creeping flush up my spine which could so easily stain my cheeks to vivid rose. There was a pause until he continued, 'I've every faith in Doctor Zane's opinion which is that the stress of the occasion must have been too much for your highly-strung temperament—'

I gave a false short laugh. 'Of course. I knew it would be that.'

'And how did you know?'

'Because he'd made up his mind beforehand,' I answered recklessly. 'He'd been well primed.'

'Whatever are you talking about?' He jerked himself upright; a second later I too was standing, facing him. I was on the point of blurting out what I believed, but realising that to bring his wife into the affair at that point would be useless, and only turn him against me, I prevaricated clumsily, saying, 'A concoction—a draught of something was given to me to drink before I went on the stage. It was the stage-manager—it was supposed to steady me, the potion I mean. But it could have been something else, couldn't it?—And suppose he knew the doctor—' I paused briefly then continued quickly, almost swallowing my

98

words, '—There's a lot of jealousy among the cast, and I kind of sensed that one or two didn't like me—' Oh, what a mess I was making of everything, I thought, suddenly breaking off.

Rupert shook his head slowly, a look of disbelief and pity on his face.

'My dear girl, what you lack in stage-discipline, you certainly make up for in imagination. The whole idea is quite ridiculous. No, please don't try such absurd excuses on me—'

'*Excuses*?' I echoed hotly. 'I'm not trying to excuse myself. Why should I? I was a failure and that's all that matters. I'm sorry you should have wasted time and money on me, but I'll repay you somehow. There's no point in talking about it any more. I said you wouldn't believe me. So please—' I swallowed painfully.

'Yes, Josephine? Please what?'

His voice had softened. He put both hands on my shoulders. I turned my face away, and tried to free myself before I weakened and flung myself into his arms. I longed to—God knows I did. But pride and fear he'd despise me, made me fight.

'Let me go,' I said brokenly. 'That's all. Let me go!'

He did so immediately.

'Certainly. I've no taste for your dramatics.'

I walked away from him, brushed a lock of hair from my forehead, made a pretence of tidying a ribbon at my bodice, then turned, cheeks flaming, and regarded him with what I hoped was a touch of dignity.

His expression was stony except for a small line of hurt bewilderment creasing from his forehead to the high bridge of his nose.

'I'm sorry,' I blurted out. 'I didn't mean—'

'No need to apologise. I should be the one to do that for daring to touch you.'

'But—'

'No buts, either, Miss Lebrun. You've made your position perfectly clear, it will take only a few minutes to explain mine. Do sit down again, it discomforts me seeing you stand so accusingly before me.' Weakly I obeyed.

'Now!—' He walked to the window, hands behind his back, then turned sharply, and continued in remote cool tones as though addressing a stranger or business acquaintance, 'I shall, of course, apologise to Signor Luigi on your behalf, and offer compensation to him for what may be taken by the public as a serious misjudgement of talent on his part. Whether he will accept it or not I can't say. In your favour, I shall point out how rushed arrangements were for you to play Lucy at such short notice, and that we all knowingly took the risk. Your youth and inexperience will be taken into account, I'm sure. He is a fair man, but under the circumstances I doubt he'll accept you as a protégée any longer. In fact, I'm sure of it, which means no more lessons are forthcoming—'

'I realise that,' I interrupted, 'Of course. I shall return as soon as possible to Falmouth, and—'

'You will do nothing of the sort.'

The peremptory statement startled me. 'I don't—'

'You don't understand?' His brows lifted in mock astonishment, or was he merely play-acting? I couldn't tell. 'Then accept it as fact, Miss Lebrun. I think you'll agree when I point out that one of the conditions of my sponsorship and your tuition under Signor Luigi was that you also helped Dame Jenny in her duties at the cottage. I can't physically imprison you here, of course, but I hardly think under the circumstances you'd be so thoughtless as to walk out leaving her to shoulder all the responsibilities of Tregonnis. It was a bargain we made, and I expect you to keep to your side of it.'

I tried to speak, but he stopped me with a wave of his hand. 'No, wait until I've finished.'

Mortified, I pressed my lips firmly together and waited.

'You'd expect payment, naturally. I'm prepared to give it —and more I'm sure than you received at the various hostelries where you worked—'

I could stand no more. Ignoring his command to remain silent, I cried, 'I expect nothing. I don't want your money or your help. About Dame Jenny—yes! I see it wouldn't be fair to leave her in the lurch, and I'll be able to do more for her without those wretched singing lessons, but only until you find someone more suitable.'

'That may take quite a time,' he stated practically, 'in the meantime, whether you like it or not you'll receive a weekly sum to provide any feminine fal-als and frippery necessary.'

'I see. A servant.'

'Do you find the word offensive?'

'Of course not. But—'

'Shall we say "help"?' he suggested. 'Do you find that more agreeable?'

'Oh—!' Misery engulfed me because he was managing to put me in such a poor light. '—I don't care, call me what you like.' I turned my back on him, took a few steps to the door, turned and remarked with forced politeness, 'Is that all, sir?'

'No.' His mood changed suddenly. He strode rapidly towards me, and before I could prevent him he'd swept me up into his arms and his lips were on mine—passionate, angry, desirous lips, that left me breathless and bewildered, dizzy with my own longing and reciprocation.

Then, suddenly, it was all over. He reached for his hat from a chair, made a mock bow and remarked ironically, 'My apologies. I can promise you there will be no repetition of such a distasteful incident for you in the future. However, dear Miss Lebrun, should you ever have the chance to play Lucy Lockett again I'm sure this little—rehearsal, shall we say—may prove to be a useful experience.'

The next moment he had gone.

CHAPTER SIX

The days following my disastrous debut, though peaceful, were without inspiration or interest for me. I did my best to help Dame Jenny in her domestic routine, but she was obviously averse to my taking any initiative. Her routine was set, and she wished for no alteration. Jan, the farmer's boy, came twice a week to scrub out the floors and chop wood, and I found myself doing little more than I did when I was having lessons from Signor Luigi. As Rupert had stipulated, a weekly sum was paid to me and delivered by a servant from Kerrysmoor with Dame Jenny's salary. She counted mine out carefully and handed it to me always with the same words, 'Be grateful to have such an obliging master. It's good money for a maid such as thee.'

What exactly her statement implied I don't know, but I don't think she meant it in any derogatory sense. Once, when I was feeling particularly moody and depressed, she remarked with a touch of concern, 'I've not heard thee sing lately. Haven't you any voice left, or is it a fit of sulks? Sulks do nothing to raise the spirits. And maybe with a little practice you could start trillin' 'gain like a bird. It's the time for it—with all the spring flowers pushing through and the sweet air blowin'.'

Yes, no one knew that more than I. A sight of or one word from Rupert Verne might have brought a burst of music from my throat, but cast off as I felt myself to be, I hadn't the heart. So I answered. 'I don't feel like it. What's the use?'

'There's use in everything if you do the best you can with it,' she told me sharply, and the irritation in her voice caused a quick movement of her head which set the bright rings flashing from her ears, and a quivering glitter of all the jewellery she wore. 'You're getting dull, girl—stir yourself up. There's always a job waiting for useful hands. What about the garden? No touching my roses, of course—I've told thee that before. But weeds are springing up as quick as mushrooms. You could lend a hand there. Thee should know a weed from a flower by now.'

'All right,' I agreed, 'yes, I can do that.'

So on a day when no wind stirred the countryside and a faint bluish haze lifted gradually above the earth and rising moors, I took a trowel and fork from the tool shed at the back of the cottage, and set to work pulling and digging carefully where unwanted wild plants threatened to thrive and smother the old

104

Lady's cherished herbs and blooms. The air was sweet and faintly damp, and as the sun brightened, golden rays caught a froth of blossom on an ancient apple tree. Occasionally a bird's rich twitter broke the silence.

After a period of bending and kneeling I stood up to ease my back, shaking the soil from my apron, and pushing the tumbled curls from my forehead. I paused, staring across the pool to its far side, where daises starred a patch of lawn. The extreme quiet was almost uncanny. In the distance the Three Maidens—no longer quite so menacing in the morning light, were touched to transient gold flame, and I visualised Kerrysmoor in the dip below hidden by its curve of the hill where Rupert would be up and about, and his lady wife perhaps still lazing in her luxurious boudoir.

Rupert.

Something in me stirred and came to life painfully. If I'd thought he'd never really cared about me at all, the ache wouldn't have hurt so acutely, but in the beginning he had—I was sure of it. Not sufficiently though to want me as a failure, an embarrassment to his friendship with Luigi, and the theatrical world. I was perhaps exaggerating; Exeter was not London, and probably I hadn't been important enough to cause even a word of criticism or derision anywhere except perhaps in a limited local press. Very well. I had to accept it; I was no use to him, except as assistance to Dame Jenny, and for keeping an eye on his precious treasures, including the mysterious portrait of the lovely girl.

I glanced down into the pool where small silver and gold fish darted through the glossy leaves of water lilies and pale spreading fern-like plants. A frail breath of air shivered over the surface causing circles of light to ebb and flow in a myriad of reflected shapes including my own face, which for an instant appeared to be that of another—of the girl who could be alive or dead, but who still haunted my imagination every time I glimpsed her limpid eyes staring at me from the heavy frame.

Nothing, for the moment, seemed quite real. Everything around me held a secret other-world atmosphere that for the first time since the disastrous *Beggar's Opera* episode, took my mind from that wretched business to different channels. I recalled the day I'd climbed the area round Rosecarrion and seen the vessel in the shadows of the narrow creek, then the other occasion—twice—when dots of human forms in the far distance had appeared momentarily and disappeared again. Perhaps I'd been mistaken in thinking I'd recognised Rupert on the boat. But if I'd been right, was the 'matter of business' he'd more than once referred to concerning his apparent avoidance of Tregonnis, something to do with contraband? And could the latter be the true cause for making the moor there forbidden territory?

During my time at Falmouth, contact with sailors and merchants had taught me much about smuggling. As a child I'd learned to accept it almost as a way of life for some—a trade frequently indulged in by the rich, and conveniently ignored by certain members of the Preventative. Agreements were often made in taverns, and taprooms of inns and kiddleywinks. Following my father's death I'd listened avidly to plots being hatched with knowing looks and snide remarks passed both in French and English. Tragedies—stories of shootings resulting in death were not uncommon. Mostly the Preventative men were loyal to their calling, but bribery often played a large part in the success or failure of an illegal operation.

Swift as lightning the question flashed through my brain. Was Rupert Verne entirely the conventional well-bred gentleman he appeared to be? Or was that merely a daytime front, a facade to hide a more dangerous daring side of his character. This could be. If so it would explain much—the adventurous gleam in his strange amber eyes—the quick flash of desire and challenge roused unexpectedly through a chance word or incident. He could be a man to whom fresh challenge was the breath of life. And I had been a part of it. He'd thought to create a legend of me—through my voice and looks expand his own dream of self-expression. Likewise in outwitting the law, he would be proving master of circumstance and other men.

Freedom! Beneath the elegant front surely was a rebellious spirit, equal to my own—as wild as the gales and storm-swept granite shores—as live and unquenchable as the impulse in me that all my life until so very recently had stirred me to joy and tears and the sweet fulfilment of song.

'Oh Rupert, Rupert,' I thought, as I turned my gaze from the pool towards the moorland ridge, 'why did you have to marry that proud iceberg of a woman? Why couldn't I have lain in your arms at night feeling our bodies close in passion—abandoned and rich in love?'

With the tangy sweet air soft and sensuous against my cheeks, I could imagine the touch of his flesh against mine—the oneness of giving and taking—a throbbing unity bred from the very heart of Nature itself. Even as I stood there my senses thrilled in wild anticipation; I released my wealth of dark curls, and loosened my bodice at the neck. Just for a brief interim the whole world seemed to sing, and a treble of music broke briefly from my throat.

Then, suddenly, I remembered.

The moments of ecstasy passed. Sober commonsense replaced the dream. I was Josephine Lebrun, servant to Dame Jenny, employed by the Master of Kerrysmoor who insisted on paying me for my services, although most of what he gave was put away in a drawer, so that when the appropriate time came and other help could be found for the old lady I would be able to return the money, either by messenger or in person, with the words, 'Thank you so much, sir, your ladyship—for the charity so kindly offered. I'm glad to have been of use, but I really do not need your gold.'

Yes; the latter method of repayment would give me the greater satisfaction—to lift my chin arrogantly at Lady Verne's cold countenance, savour the amazed astonishment in her narrowed eyes and on her thin lips. During the brief occasions we'd met so far she'd used every subtle means to insult me, but one day, I told myself, my pride alone would defeat her.

'A princess,' Pierre had told me so often. 'You are my princess. Never forget that, *ma chère*.' Remembering now, urged me into a gentler mood. It was as though a smoothing hand and voice from the past were resurrected momentarily lulling conflicting emotions to reason and renewed confidence.

Presently I went back into the cottage. The sky had darkened slightly, bringing a train of cloud from the west. A faint breeze stirred the stillness taking the frail hazed sunlight behind a veil of grey.

'Shouldn't be surprised if we had a storm later,' Dame Jenny said when I walked into the kitchen. 'There was the smell of rain about in the early hours.'

'That will be good for your garden, won't it?'

'S'long as it doesn't beat my roses down,' she replied guardedly.

She needn't have feared. When evening came only misted rain fell, clearing sufficiently to give at intervals a glimmer of blurred moonlight. A strange, nostalgic kind of night, reminding me again of times long ago, when as a child I'd waited by Falmouth harbour searching the waters for the sight of a ship emerging from a grey horizon with my father at the helm. Perhaps it was the atmosphere that made me restless, but I had an impulse to go wandering—to climb Rosecarrion and explore the territory above the creek—to find out for myself if the boat had left, or was still there. Commonsense told me that it would hardly have remained inactive since my first glimpse of it. Instinct, though, was stranger than commonsense. I just knew something was going on that concerned Rupert Verne; moreover the misty scene moon-washed one moment, the next darkened by cloud, was exactly right for a successful smuggling operation—yet could bewilder the Preventative men with its constantly changing shadowed shapes—of rocks, twisted trees and bushes crouching towards the water above jagged thrusting cliffs.

I took a close look at Dame Jenny, who was busy with her needle by the fire. Although springtime, the nights could still be chilly, and that morning Jan had brought logs, so a cheerful blaze enabled her to concentrate comfortably, with the aid of an oil lamp on the table. I knew though that she was getting sleepy, and was not surprised when she said, 'I'll be going to my bed early tonight, girl, and I advise you to do the same. There'll be baking to do tomorrow, and ironing of the aprons and caps.'

'Don't worry,' I said, 'I'm quite capable of baking bread and buns now, and the ironing's nothing. Still, I'll do as you say. There's the garden too.'

She scrutinised me sharply from her small bright eyes.

'Tired thee, did it?—The weedin' and diggin'?'

'Not really,' I said. 'I just feel comfortably lazy.'

I didn't like lying to her, but I knew very well that if she'd the least inkling of my plan when she was safely asleep, she'd put a stop to it, and it would be very difficult to get a second chance. So I put on an air of placidity which beguiled her into retiring early, while I made my way to my own bedroom.

I waited for over an hour before opening my door and tip-toeing along the short landing to her room which overlooked the lane. Pressing my ear to the keyhole I was reassured by the distinct rhythmical sound of her snoring, which indicated she had taken her dose of hot

111

toddy, and would probably sleep innocently through the night.

The rest, though tricky, was not really difficult. Wearing a cape over my clothes, and with my boots in one hand I crept softly downstairs, unlatched the kitchen window which was down to the ground, and climbed cautiously out. I waited a moment, listening. There was no sound from above, no flicker of light or indication that the old lady had heard. I knew I was safe for an hour or two, and after a minute or so moved cautiously along the side of the cottage to the garden gate leading into the lane.

From there, with the hood covering my hair, head forward, I hurried, half-running, to the hill's curve where a track wound upwards, then to my right in the direction of the creek. I followed it. But finding the exact path I'd taken before was impossible in the shrouded shadows, drifting mist, and intermittent glimpses of rain-washed moonlight. Briar and thorn, twisted clumps of heather and gorse hunched by tumbled granite boulders made progress slow. But at last through a brief sudden clearance of cloud, a glimmer of sea glittered ahead, only to be taken the next moment into darkness again. I was more certain then of the exact locality, and decided to climb higher, and wend my way round the top end of the ravine—or creek, so a view—however blurred—might be possible of anything going on below.

Nearer the summit of the slope the land was more barren and free of tortuous obstructions. At a point above the ruin that I'd observed previously, I paused to look down on the gaunt cut in the rock face where the boat had been anchored. The mist and fine rain had thinned a little, leaving a grey desolate vista of land and sea. The creek was merely a gash of darkness. No ship was discernible, no sign of human life—the atmosphere was one of elemental desolation, and suddenly I felt chilled. I had been wrong then to sense adventure in which Rupert Verne might have been concerned.

Then, quite unexpectedly the moon's pale glare broke completely free of cloud and drizzle spreading luminous clarity over the landscape.

I was astonished. The boat *was* there, hunched close above the tide against the glassy black brilliance of the rock face. But it was obviously a wreck, and in the past sometime had floundered and been forsaken, which seemed odd, as vessels of that type were usually salvaged by owners or the authorities. There could be no other answer; but the question still remained concerning the male figures I'd seen on deck before, taking one to be Rupert. I had probably been mistaken, concocting an image of who I wished it to be, from an overwrought imagination.

Reluctantly, I turned and made my way

113

back to Tregonnis, but on impulse took a route passing close to the ruin. The rain had ceased now, and the mist and cloud had lifted considerably. When I neared the tumbled granite relic I guessed that generations ago it had probably been a moorland chapel, built to serve worshippers of outlying mining hamlets and farms. Methodism, still a force in Cornwall, had flourished with wild fervour then. Even John Wesley himself could have preached there. Later as certain copper mines in the district failed and families took off to the Americas or left for the North Country and employment in the cotton industry, many such buildings would have lost their use except as shelter for cattle, tramping vagabonds, or occasional dumping for smuggled goods. Yes, the latter was possible, though hardly likely to be suspect by the military, being on Verne land. And there were so many such ruins dotted about the Cornish coast. The Preventative generally had far more important business on their hands than to go searching and keeping an eye on every forsaken relic left to decay.

All the same—due to my heightened imagination, the eerie night and my concern over Rupert—stimulated by impulse and my own wild thoughts, I pushed my way through brambles, over stones and rough patches of inky damp earth, until I reached the entrance half obscured by rocks and fallen stones.

I went in.

The roof was almost completely gone. Only three walls were left standing, and the far side facing the coast was a mere wreck of fallen granite allowing the weak moonlight to streak across the rough floor. Queer shadows lurked from corners filling the interior with creeping uneasy menace. The air had a fetid, musty smell, mingled with something else—something reminiscent of certain ancient kiddleywinks I'd once known in childhood. Whisky. Was it whisky I could smell? Had some drunken vagabond been spending an hour or two there with his bottle? I felt the skin tighten about the back of my neck and skull. Was that dark lump in the far corner that of a human being—dead perhaps? I wanted to turn and leave the sinister place, but curiosity forbade me.

I went forward cautiously, keeping my eyes on the ground, half feeling my way, and in a wanton beam of moonlight I discovered that the floor was flagged. Well, of course, it would be if the place had ever been a chapel or part of a mine house.

Then I had a surprise. My heart and pulses jerked. Near the open wall facing the coast, slabs had been moved, and it appeared to me, fairly recently. There was a gap of darkness—empty darkness—between two, that suggested an underground tunnel of some constructed foundation below. Earth had been dislodged and had not yet settled. Someone had been there.

I stood, puzzled, forgetful of how chilled I was becoming, of the passing of time, or that Dame Jenny might soon be stirring. It was very rarely in the night she did so, but there was always a slight chance; nothing registered in my thoughts though save the mounting excitement I'd *discovered* something.

I bent down to examine the dislodged flagstone, and then I heard it—the thud, thud of horses' hooves coming nearer—nearer— just as though the wild black horseman of the Cornish moors—of the legendary Devil's Carn—was riding to seize me. I'd read stories about him in my youth, most Cornish folk had; but until that moment I'd had no fear, had felt only a pleasurable stirring excitement.

Now I knew why the myth had arisen. Were the sounds *really* those of a rider of the night? Or due to some strange elemental manifestation that could be explained by a naturalist or geological expert? I waited with my ears strained, listening. Louder and louder. Thud, thud, thud. The hollow sound seemed to reverberate underfoot and through the air. There could be no mistake about it—whether demon or man, the rider—or could it be some wild stallion rampaging on its own?—was making for the ruin.

Tensely I pushed my spine rigidly against the damp granite wall. Seconds passed, and then suddenly the thudding ceased; there was a

116

snorting and neighing, a murmuring of a male voice, and rattle of metal or reins; a moment later a dark form pushed through the ruined doorway, kicking and striking stones with his boots as he approached.

Then he paused.

Except for the drip of water trickling from between granite bricks, no sound penetrated the short silence that followed. The weird lemon light struck sideways on his face, accentuating the deep carved lines of it, dominant nose, thrusting jaw, and the glint of yellow eyes under heavy brows.

Rupert.

I waited for him to speak first; the seconds seemed interminable.

Then, as though from a dream, I heard him say in deadly calm tones, 'What are *you* doing here?'

Unable to concoct a satisfactory answer— well, what *could* be satisfactory under such conditions?—I blurted out, 'I was just poking round. I was curious.'

He still didn't attempt to touch me.

'Obviously. And what right do you think you have? On *my* land, on such a night, at such a time, and when you've expressly been forbidden to come this way at all?'

My nerve began to return, and with it a welling-up of my quick temper.

'None, of course. Since coming to Tregonnis, I seem to have given up all the rights I ever had. But for once I wanted to feel free and take a bit of a wander without being watched or told where to go. Oh I know you've been very kind to me—in a way—paying for my lessons with that fiery little Italian—forcing me into a—a—debut I wasn't ready for on that beastly Exeter stage—letting me make a fool of myself, and then turning me into some sort of servant to that funny old lady. Your wife, too!—she hates me—you can see it in her eyes, her manner, and the way she lifts her long nose every time we meet!—and why—*why*?' I broke off, breathless, but somehow relieved to get it all out.

'*You* know why,' he said, and his voice was meaningful, a little unsteady and harsh.

The moon had slipped behind cloud again. Everything was damp darkness, filled with lurking shadows, strange and exciting, pulsing with all the hidden secret forces of that Cornish night. The ground squelched underfoot as he took one stride towards me. A bramble caught his sleeve.

He tore his arm free, and suddenly it was round me, taking my body close to his; his lips were warm against my neck, mouth and damp shoulder and breast where the cloak had fallen away. I struggled a little, then let my head fall and lie against him. How heavily his heart beat, and how wonderful it was to hear its steady thumping—strong with the urge and longing of life.

118

'You know very well why,' he murmured again.

I could feel the hardening of him, and felt response rise in me. I wanted to cry, 'Love me. Rupert, oh, love me—' but he forced me from him gently, firmly.

'Hardly an ideal place for such—indiscretions,' he said, with an attempt of lighthearted mockery. He sighed, folded his arms, and continued in more level tones, 'Now what the devil am I going to do with you? For you're a witch if ever there was one.'

'Not all witches are bad,' I answered, trying to match my mood to his. At that moment the moon must have slipped out from behind the clouds again. The dark walls lightened to eerie bluish green, giving a radiance and brief clarity to the scene which before had been a mere background of shadow, and in those first few seconds I happened to glance down and noticed once more the line between slab and dislodged earth. Quick as lightning his gaze followed mine.

'Your bright eyes are observant, I note.' The dry tone was back in his voice. 'I might have known you'd miss nothing.'

'Was it important I should?'

'Yes,' he answered. 'Knowing my business is hardly your affair—living as you are. And I have never made a habit of sharing any of my male interests with women—'

'I'm not just *women* I'm—'

'I know, I know. You're a deuced aggravating, inquisitive little baggage who's managed to steal a march on me in every way—first as a singer, then as an intriguing young woman, and now as a would-be pirate.'

'Pirate?' I gasped.

He laughed.

'What you suspect *me* of being—smuggler.'

'I—'

'Which I am,' he interrupted. 'Oh, I'm not going to deny it. What would be the use? You've already somehow got your pretty little nose on the scent. How? Why?—God knows. Maybe your training in bars and kiddleywinks. Or maybe just an uncanny sixth sense—something peculiarly special between the two of us.' His manner changed, softened. 'Is that it, Josephine?' Through the fitful light his eyes searched mine—narrow golden eyes warm with desire and tenderness.

'I think it must be,' I admitted, 'but I didn't *know*. You needn't have told me. You see—' Words quickened from my lips '—I'd seen things from my window at Tregonnis. Not as far as this, of course—but a man, walking—half crawling at times along the hill as though—as though—' I broke off, continuing quickly, 'Well, I thought the first time it was a miner going home, but there isn't a mine just there, is there? And then once or twice I went for a walk—'

'*Ah.*'

'—Where you'd told me not to, and I found the creek where the boat was, the old wreck. I didn't connect you exactly, not then. But the next time I went further, and saw figures on the deck. They weren't very clear, it was some distance away; all the same—I was certain you were one of them. And it seemed funny; I wondered what you were doing—'

'As I thought. And tonight you decided to investigate.'

'Something like that.'

'Why?—Why tonight?'

'I've told you, I was bored by being kept on a string, and wanted to be free.'

He threw out his arms and let them fall to his sides in exasperation. 'Freedom. That's all you think of—freedom. And now look what you've got into—'

'I'd *like* to look,' I said impudently.

'Then you'll have to be disappointed,' he replied promptly. 'And I mean it. You'll do what you're told, and believe me when I inform you that even if I made the effort to remove that slab you'd find nothing in the dank dungeon below, but a load of rubbish and mud and snails—don't you realise, my love, that a clever villain like myself always has an alibi? For instance it's my right to hunt prowling poachers on a dark night? So don't go airing stupid ideas. No one would believe your word against Master Verne's.'

'The smell of spirits *is* very strong,' I pointed

121

out, impertinently.

He shook his head, and grasped my arm. 'Come along, Miss Lebrun. Time for quizzing and play-acting is done. I'm taking you back to Tregonnis as quickly as Flash can make it, and I repeat, not a word of this, you understand? Then in the morning what's left of it—you'll tell yourself all your strange imaginings were just a dream.'

'You're saying—you didn't really mean it?'

'Mean what?'

'When you kissed me,' I said bluntly.

For answer he slipped his arm round me and said gently, 'Yes, I meant it. And one day—'

'One day?' I prompted.

'We'll have to see, won't we, how things work out?'

It wasn't the answer I'd wanted, but it sufficed.

The next moment, still with his hand on my arm he was leading me from the ruin to the stump of a tree where his stallion, Flash, was tethered.

So it was that we rode together that night under a belt of thin cloud—lovers not yet free to love openly, but with the rich secret of passion between us that I knew must one day be revealed.

Dame Jenny was still safely in her bedroom when I pushed the kitchen window open and climbed over the sill.

I removed my boots, crept up the stairs and

into my room, not waiting to listen for any slight sound from the old lady's bedroom. It must have been one o'clock by then. For some time excitement and a sense of wild fulfilment kept me awake. But at last I slept, and when morning came it was fine, and a blackbird was trilling from somewhere near my window.

I wanted to sing too. For the first time since the Exeter disaster I thought it possible I would.

And all because Rupert had kissed me and in a careless moment called me his love.

CHAPTER SEVEN

A week following my moorland adventure I went down to the kitchen one morning and found Dame Jenny lying on the floor. She was a pathetic sight, with her old face twisted to one side, and a broken cup shattered by one jewelled hand. An earring had been knocked off, and her mob cap fallen, taking her hair with it. I hadn't known she wore a wig, and the sight of her so defenceless and very ancient, moved me to pity.

I managed to lift her up somehow and ease her into her favourite chair. She made an effort to say something, but what I couldn't tell, the words were unintelligible. Luckily it was a day when Jan called with wood, and as soon as he arrived I sent him to Kerrysmoor with a message of what had happened.

Then I made her a hot drink and waited, holding her hand. I wasn't terribly surprised at her collapse; for some time I'd noticed that she was gradually failing. Her hands had shaken more under the slightest stress, and she'd been inclined to 'get in a tizzy' over nothing. Her walk had lost its lightness, and she'd been mislaying things in the house more and more frequently. It was clear to me she'd suffered a stroke, and I hoped her high-and-mighty ladyship wouldn't want the poor old thing to be carted away to an institution.

I needn't have worried.

When the doctor had been, and delivered his verdict, which was the same as mine, Rupert told me to pack Dame Jenny's valise with all that was necessary, while he carried the old lady outside.

'And you'd better include her reticule and jewel box,' he said. 'Her stay at Kerrysmoor may be a prolonged one, but obviously it's the best place for her.'

I did what he said and in a matter of less than half an hour the frail old lady was being carefully deposited in the waiting chaise with the help of the doctor. Rupert came back for a moment before leaving.

'You're not afraid to remain here alone, I hope? At least for a day or two. After that possibly it can be arranged for a servant from the house to be installed here as company. Here's a pistol—' he handed me one carefully, '—in case any unwelcome visitors should appear. It's loaded, but the safety catch is on. You know how to use it, I presume?' His voice had a questioning note, the narrowed eyes were anxious.

I lifted my head boldly. 'I'm afraid of no intruder, sir, and yes, I *do* know how to handle it, if necessary. There's no need to worry about me at all, or to send a servant down. I shall be quite all right.'

His lips closed in a tight line. 'That's for me to say.'

I flushed. The look he gave me was dark, a little forbidding and commanding. 'You may be very courageous,' he continued after a brief pause, 'but you are somewhat—unpredictable—and a great deal of wealth is stored here. For some time I thought added protection was advisable, so in the meantime, until we make more permanent arrangements, I shall insist on you having a dog—Brutus—who is a trained guard, but a faithful affectionate hound and friend to those in his charge. He's well-known to Jan who'll be given instructions to bring food over once every day, and to give the animal regular exercise. Tomorrow Jan will collect him from Kerrysmoor and bring him along. In a very short time, I can assure you, you'll be firm friends.'

125

'I hope so,' I said rather primly.

His mood changed in the unexpected way I was becoming accustomed to.

'Josephine—' the tentative flicker of a smile touched his lips, 'don't entirely neglect your singing. I have faith in your voice, and still believe that one day, perhaps, its quality will be recognised.'

'Oh!' I laughed artificially. 'What does my *voice* matter?'

'To me it does. And when I look in one day to see how things are with you and Brutus, I hope I shall have the privilege of hearing it.'

So polite and formal; yet my heart leaped through hearing that he would be visiting Tregonnis.

'Well—' he stood uncertainly for a moment, while I wondered wildly if he'd kiss me. But he didn't. He merely touched my hand, gave a slight bow, and was gone.

Of course, I told myself, as the chaise started off down the road, he'd been afraid lest the doctor's shrewd eyes should notice any slight intimacy between us.

Etiquette!

How stupid that feelings had to be disguised under a mask of manners. But *were* his rare passionate lapses deep and true as mine were?—or was he playing a little side-game with me? Keeping me on a string for his own ends? How did I *know*? Men, my stepmother used to tell me, were false feckless creatures, and the more highly born, the more deviously cunning their motives could be. But then she'd had no standing and put no value on herself or her body; perhaps if Pierre had lived—the question didn't arise though. I knew deep down she would have eventually betrayed him. And I was sad remembering how my father had trusted her.

Looking back too intensely can bring its worries, and at that moment, as I recalled Pierre, I wondered what his advice would have been at this exact point in my life—to follow love where I knew it lay, and grasp it with both hands and all the will and strength I had?—Or to cut adrift and seek fulfilment somewhere else in some other fashion? I still had my voice. There was nothing in the world now to stop me walking out, and wandering the wild sweet lanes of summer where blossom foamed about the hedges and lush bluebells grew.

Rupert, after all, was a married man with a stately home and a noble wife. He was bound by ties which would not easily be broken. I was an intruder into his heart—as he was in mine. But I was mistress of my own destiny, whereas he was not of his, and unless his love was as strong and all-consuming as mine, any future between us would be ignoble and wrong. Yes, I knew I was right in my judgement there, and that Pierre would have said the same. Of this I was certain, and with the certainty something in me that had been reckless and immature grew up and brought me to a calmer mood.

I would stay at Tregonnis for the time being, I decided; this was only fair considering the arrangements that were being made concerning the dog, and there being no one else to guard Rupert's treasure room. But later—I sighed. How futile it was to make plans when I'd no idea *exactly* of what others were being made for me. Already my thoughts were becoming too involved to view rationally. So I cleared my mind of all problems, and decided to have a breath of air in the garden. As I passed down the short hall I noticed that the door of the treasure room was slightly ajar; Dame Jenny must have been looking round before she collapsed.

I fetched the key and was about to close and lock it, when I thought I heard a sound. I stepped inside and had a glance round. No one was there; the faint creaking could have been of old wood, a floor board, or draught of air playing about the figurines. A slanting beam of sunlight quivered over glass, giving life to the delicate miniatures in their black velvet mounts and gold frames. Shadows made a fine tracery over rugs and up walls; the slightest movement of cloud or drifting light from outside lit the crystal and glass to momentary shivering brilliance. It was as though for a few brief moments the interior came alive and I stood in a world of fantasy and bygone luxury.

I glanced towards the fireplace. The girl in

the portrait stared down at me with a serene sweet-sad half-smile on her lips.

'I wish I knew all about you,' I thought, 'I wish I knew who you were, and what part you played in Rupert's life.'

It did not occur to me as strange just then, that I should think of her in the past tense, or connect her so personally with Rupert. Was I jealous? Perhaps. Jealous because her place there was obviously of great importance, and cherished above all the other contents of that secret domain. I had sensed it from my first day at Tregonnis, a feeling that had been endorsed by Rupert's refusal to talk of her, and Dame Jenny's irate snub when I'd asked for information.

As I turned and went out, locking the door behind me, I realised fully, for the first time, what a world of mystery and adventure I'd become involved in since leaving Falmouth. Rupert!—the smuggling—Signor Luigi—the terrible theatrical experience—even Lady Verne's peculiar animosity towards me, and the secret room dominated by the picture of the beautiful unknown girl.

The pistol also. I hadn't been quite honest with Rupert when I'd told him I knew how to use it. It was just that during my life at the inn I'd seen firearms threateningly wielded and had once even witnessed a duel, unknown to my stepmother. I was a little surprised that Mr Verne should have trusted me with such a

129

weapon—I'd no idea that the dangerous looking object was loaded with blank bullets only and was merely for a means of frightening off any offender, and ensuring my own self-confidence.

Still, burglaries, shootings, and smuggling, seemed remote and very far away that day, as I wandered round the garden, thinking sadly of Dame Jenny. She would be cared for, yes, at Kerrysmoor, but I doubted that even if she recovered sufficiently to walk about again on her own two feet, she would ever be happy living as a dependent without her own small precious domain to reign over. And why had she been left on her own for so long, considering the responsibilities entailed as 'keeper of Tregonnis'?—Perhaps because in the eyes of many country folk and natives of Tharne she had the reputation of being some sort of a witch—a *white* witch, it was emphasised, although in the tiny village post office one day I'd heard two local women agreeing in an undertone that there was no such thing as the white kind. '*Any* witch is bound to have a bit o' dark power in her.'

So her quaint eccentricities—jewels, fineries, diminutive stature and her herbs had probably been her protection. Even her roses might have added to the superstition; they were certainly extremely lush, over-large, and beautiful, and that morning their scent hung sweetly and particularly powerfully in the summer air.

Their velvet petalled colour—flame, yellow, and deep dark crimson filled the whole of one wide border at the side of the pool; a few petals drifted on the shining water. It was indeed as though a magical hand had brushed the terrain. Or were such thoughts merely crowding my mind because I was so completely alone, and shocked by the niggling thought that the old lady might never see her beloved blossoms again?

I was looking forward to meeting Brutus, and hoped very much that the following day when Jan called for him at Kerrysmoor Rupert also might decide to come along. I spent a little time in the garden, reluctant somehow to go immediately back into the cottage which would be an empty place without the old lady. In a strange way I'd grown fond of her—the thought of the quaint interior—silent except for the ticking of the old clock and occasional tinkle from the treasure room when a waft of air drifted against mobile crystal, was melancholy. So I wandered first to the very end of Tregonnis land, which looked over a small buttercup field before rising to the rough patch of moor.

'You needn't bother trying to weed over there,' Dame Jenny had told me more than once. 'No proper flowers grow in that thick scrub. All brambles and holes and stones it is. A real rubbish dump of its kind. One day I'll have Jan clear it and cut some of the thorns down. You could get all kinds of wild animal critters sneakin' there. Once there was a fox had its hole nearby. Things used to disappear from the pantry—cheese, eggs—anything eatable there was and I just couldn't understand how—until one mornin' I saw the fox streakin' across the field. Then I knew. Must get rid of *that*, I said to myself. And I did. That very evening.'

'Do you mean you had it shot or something?' I'd questioned her.

She'd looked shocked.

'My dear life, I wouldn't do such a thing to a livin' critter however wicked it might be. Oh *no*, my dear.' She'd paused and added, 'I have other means of getting rid of unwelcome visitors.'

'How?'

'That's *my* secret,' she'd said smugly, with a little nod of the head that had sent the bright earbobs shaking beneath her mob cap. I'd known then why the natives were suspicious of the old lady.

I was recalling the incident, when I pushed the briars away that morning following her collapse and departure. The smothering undergrowth, indeed, could provide effective coverage for many small wild creatures. I found a sturdy stick—part of a branch torn from a tree—and started beating the thorny barrier down. It wasn't easy, and perhaps I was stupid to bother; my hand and wrist got badly

132

scratched, and an end of my pinafore was ripped. However, as I neared what remained of a half-tumbled fence, my curiosity was roused by a roundish dark patch covered by trailing weeds and thorn indicating there might be a hole or vacuum below.

I bent forward for a closer look, and poked the stick through the tangle of smothering intertwined branches. The ground beneath was hollow. It took me sometime to manipulate sufficient space to peer down, and what I saw sent a shiver of excitement through me. At first glimpse I thought it was a shaft of an old mine, then I realised it was not quite wide enough. It could only have been a well then, at some time. But if so—why was there no water in it now? All I could see was blackness vanishing into the dark earth, and obviously it had been originally man-made. On one side near the surface, granite bricks jutted out almost like steps.

I screwed my eyes up trying to get a more accurate view, but it was impossible. So presently I straightened up, dusted small twigs and leaves from my hair, shook my skirt and damaged apron, and after lightly replacing some of the weedy tendrils and branches, turned to go back into the cottage. Why I'd bothered to cover the hole again I didn't know; it had probably been as it was for years, and was of no real significance any more. I suppose I was simply trying to divert my mind from poor Dame Jenny's plight, by filling my imagination with other problems—making a mystery of something that in reality was no mystery at all.

The cottage seemed a solitary place when I went in.

I found myself eagerly looking forward to the next day, when Jan was to bring the dog to Tregonnis, accompanied—hopefully—by Rupert.

But when morning came only Jan and Brutus arrived. The master, the youth told me had sent a message saying he'd probably call at the end of the week.

My heart sank.

Probably. Sterile comfort indeed considering how passionately I longed to see him. Under a veneer of brightness, however, I covered my disappointment, and enquired about Dame Jenny.

'She'm a bit better, Miss, so I've heard tell,' Jan replied. 'In bed o' course. Well, she would be wouldn' she, an old wumman like her, after such a turn—you'd've thought she'd've managed to avoid such things—her with all that grand knowledge she do have—'

I supposed he was referring to her reputed mystic powers, and was about to make some trite reply when the dog, a golden labrador, prevented me by getting up on his hind legs and giving an affectionate lick on my chin.

'He likes you a'ready. That he do,' Jan

134

remarked. 'You've got a friend, that's for sure.'
And I had.

Quite soon he'd fitted into his new routine
and seemed to know from the start he was there
for my protection. His bark was fearsome to
strangers, but few visited Tregonnis, unless it
was a pedlar or someone from the farm, and on
such occasions a word from me would silence
him and bring him to heel. Occasionally, if I
went for a stroll, I'd allow him to accompany
me, but only for a short time. He was, after all,
sole guardian of the cottage and its treasures
during my absence, and Rupert would have
been annoyed if he'd called and found neither
of us there.

But he didn't call, and I became restless and
resentful—tired of being bound to the country
through duties I hadn't willingly undertaken.
Mysteries of smuggling, secret rooms, legends,
and having long hours alone to ponder and
brood on the past and the uncertain future,
frequently irritated me to a point almost
beyond endurance. I would long then for the
colourful steamy excitement of the Golden
Bird—to be whirling round in my coloured
skirts and shawls, dancing and singing—
always singing—with faces transfixed before
me, blurred discs of watchfulness through the
smoky musty air.

More than once I impetuously packed my
valise, ready to disappear leaving a note for
Rupert Verne, saying:

I'm sorry, being caretaker doesn't suit me. Thank you for all you've done for me, but as I've failed in becoming a great singer like you wanted, I'm going somewhere where I can be myself and let my voice do just what it feels like. I did love you, Mr Verne, but my sort of love isn't what you need.

Yours respectfully,

Josephine Lebrun.

Once I even went so far as to put on my bonnet and cape, and leave the note on the small table in the hall. Then Brutus's bark from the scullery where he slept, made me change my mind, and I went inside again. It wasn't fair to leave the dog alone. Supposing Jan for some reason didn't call in the morning? The poor thing would be left without food or company for goodness knows how long.

The thought of Rupert himself, too, from a niggle at the back of my mind, came to life again. He must *one* day call at Tregonnis, and I needed to be there when it happened—to make him realise how his neglect—and surely it *was* neglect, considering the passion of his kisses and meaningful glances of his eyes, the many many avowals of unspoken love—had hurt me! and angered, too. Oh yes, I was angry. Before perhaps I'd had no rightful cause to show it. But now I had. I would *not* be treated like any rich man's cheap little plaything to be flattered one moment, bullied the next, then pushed into oblivion just when he felt like it.

During my period of waiting for Rupert's possible visit, I rehearsed the scene several times—how I would greet him in a dignified fashion telling him of my decision to leave Tregonnis, of my intention to make my own career—even inventing another vague sponsor anxious to promote my voice. The latter would be a lie, of which Pierre no doubt would have disapproved. But for once I didn't care. I would be *me*! my words would be haughty, my gaze cold and remote. I even practised the lift of head and manner of addressing him before my looking glass. And I was careful these days always to appear my best in my most attractive clothes, and do my housework mostly at nights when I would not be caught on my knees in my working calico dress under a long apron.

Oh yes! I made what I imagined were all necessary preparations for the longed-for event. But, of course, when it happened, as is so often the case—everything was completely unexpected.

The morning had been windless but damp, with fine rain turning to fitful mist by afternoon. Twilight, later, hung a grey shroud over the horizon of moors and sky. Steamy rivulets of moisture hugged the windows of Tregonnis; every slight sound there was from outside seemed intensified—the drip, drip of wet leaves from bushes, crying of a gull and flap of wings as it rose into the air, the scuttering rustle of some wild creatures through the undergrowth—and something else—something sensed rather than heard, an uneasiness that seemed itself an entity, chilling my blood. A more practical person would have called it imagination, but Brutus was aware of it, and several times lifted his head as though alerted to danger. Twice a low growl came from his throat. He left the rug by the hearth and went to the door, then returned and lay down again, stretched out, head on paws, but with eyes watchful, tense.

I laid my needlwork aside, lit the oil lamp and went to the window to draw the sittingroom curtains. Intuitively I glanced out towards the west. It was almost dark, but as I paused there briefly a dot of light flashed for a second, then was gone. It could have been a shepherd's lantern perhaps, I told myself reasoningly, although it had appeared over-brilliant for that, and would not so quickly have been snuffed out. It was about to move when I saw it again, only a pinpoint on the moor, somewhere to my far right in the direction of my walks around Rosecarrion. The second flash was quickly followed by a sharp crack of sound like that of a shot being fired. Brutus sprang to his feet and came towards me.

'It's all right, down boy! down!' I said, and pulled the blinds together with a rattle. Then I returned to my chair. For a time the dog was

138

restless, but when no further noise followed, he eventually settled. I crossed once or twice to the window again; everything was dark, muted grey, showing no sign of life or movement. Yet in my bones still I felt something was astir; and when I went to bed made sure that the pistol was beside me on the small table by my side.

I closed my eyes, hoping to get to sleep early and that no troubled dreams would disturb my rest. It was no use. Brutus, who slept in the hall, was uneasy, and at one point gave a mournful howl followed by a low growl and bark. I went to the top of the stairs and gave the command used by Jan to quieten him. For a time it seemed to work. All was silent except for the thickening steady drip of rain that had intensified during the past hour.

Then, suddenly, there was a wild yelling and barking from the animal, together with a frantic pounding of paws against the wooden door.

I jumped out of bed, flung a wrap round my shoulders, and ran downstairs.

'Quiet!' I called to the dog, 'What's the matter? Whatever's got into you—?'

He was standing on his hind legs, paws against the wooden surface, and didn't obey me when I told him to, 'Come back and be a good boy'. He gave a further yelp, turned his head towards me, and I saw then his excitement was partly pleasure. The limpid eyes were alight, his tail was wagging wildly;

his whole attitude was of supplication.

No animal could have begged more obviously, 'Open it, open the door.'

I paused for a moment, uncertain, apprehensive.

And then I heard it—a man's voice and a hammering against the wood—'For God's sake let me in—it's me—Rupert.'

With my heart quickening and thumping painfully, I rushed to both bolts, drew them, and turned the key in the lock, and pulled the door wide.

Half staggering and breathing heavily, Rupert Verne plunged into the hall. He was wet and hatless. Rain from his dark hair ran down his face, mingling with the trickle of blood from one temple. I tried to steady him, but he waved me aside, and with the dog nosing about his legs and feet, blundered into the parlour. In the glow of the lamp his face appeared drawn and haggard, and I saw also that one arm had been wounded near the shoulder. When he tried to lift it, he winced in pain.

'Sit down,' I said, although I didn't need to; before the words were out he'd slumped on to the sofa. 'I'll get you a drink.'

Knowing where the old lady kept her special toddy, I went to her secret cupboard in the kitchen, filled a wine glass full of the liquid and took it through to him. His breathing had eased; he gulped it down eagerly, sat for a moment without speaking, then laughed ruefully, and said, 'I must look a sorry sight.'

'Yes, you do,' I affirmed.

And it was true. It was not only the damp clothes and blood-stained neckscarf; mud and twigs clung to his black coat and breeches, lumps of soil tangled his hair; it was as though he'd been in an earthquake.

'What happened?' I asked. '—No, wait. You must have a wash first. Those cuts are more than scratches. Can you get your coat off?'

'If not, you'll have to saw it away, won't you?' He was trying to make light of the business, but I knew he was in pain.

I didn't wait to give reply to such a stupid remark, but went through to the kitchen, where the range was still warm from baking, and had a kettle of water on it. I poured some into a bowl, and with a clean cloth hurried back to the parlour. In my absence Rupert had managed to remove his coat. The blood was already clotting near the shoulder, and when I'd wiped it clean I saw that the wound, though nasty, was probably from where a bullet had grazed it. Superficial, thank God, like the graze near one temple; but neglected either could have given serious trouble.

How long it took for him to appear clean and in respectable shape, I don't recall. I was surprised at his submissiveness to my help. It was not until the dabbing and washing and bandaging were over that I could relax and notice his expression.

There was a little smile about his stern mouth, his long eyes were slightly crinkled at the corners. It was as though he was mildly amused. *Amused*—when I'd been so frantic with anxiety, so wrought-up and tense on his behalf.

'Thank you,' he said. 'You missed your true vocation, Miss Lebrun. You would make an excellent nurse—or should I say, you already *are* one.'

'There's no need to pay me compliments,' I said abruptly.

'I'd just like to know—'

'What I've been up to? How and why I've arrived here in such a dastardly uncivilized manner? And what the devil I'm thinking about, placing a young woman in such a compromising situation?' he interrupted. 'Of course, naturally.' He regarded me reflectively then continued after a short pause, 'There was trouble tonight near the creek—'

'Smuggling, you mean!'

'Don't hurry me. Yes, smuggling. Brandy and lace. Unfortunately a certain excise officer who in the past had been—fairly co-operative shall we say—in turning a blind eye—had been replaced for some unknown reason by a particularly odious character who'd been on bad terms with me for quite a time. When the force arrived on the scene the small boats—French—were luckily away. But the cargo

142

hadn't yet been completely cleared. My men were spotted after removing the last kegs from that old wreck you saw, to the mouth of a cave that's generally blocked by a slab. There's a tunnel there leading to the old chapel—'

'I *thought* something like that.'

Ignoring my statement he continued, 'Rosecarrion is a hive of tunnels. Very useful routes to dumping depots. You found one, when you located the old chapel so cunningly.'

'Why are you telling me all this?' I asked. 'And why—how did you arrive at the kitchen door of this cottage? I don't understand.'

He lazed back on the sofa with an enigmatic look on his face that discomforted me. It was as though he was assessing me properly for the first time, wondering whether or not he could trust me perhaps—or about something else—something deeply personal that brought the rich colour to my cheeks and set my heart racing.

'I don't think you're telling me the truth, Miss Lebrun. You understand far more than you admit. For instance—if you search my coat pocket you'll discover a shred of linen—a lady's handkerchief, I believe—that I found on a thorn bush when I struggled up those abominable steps. You knew very well there was a passage hidden below all that rubble.' He smiled wrily. 'A pity you didn't realise I'd have to use it—maybe you could have cleaned it up a little.'

Enlightenment dawned on me.

'*Oh!* the *hole.*'

'Exactly. This cottage was used in the past as a dumping place for goods. But not for many years. I needed it for—other things.' He lowered his gaze. His voice dropped a little sadly, reminding me of what 'other things' probably implied—mostly the image of the lovely girl in the portrait.

'I see.'

He sighed. 'Maybe you will eventually, and I expect you're wondering why I took that foul passage tonight?'

'Well—why did you?'

'I became a fox, Josephine, so the revenue, like hounds, could hunt *me* instead of my two faithful men, which they did. The entrance to the passage is some distance from the cove, leading from a rock crevice, just wide enough to squeeze through. Conveniently for me, the clouds thickened at the most important moment, leaving the Preventative completely bemused. Hopefully, my accomplices had sufficient time to be properly away and replace the slab. If they didn't—'

'Yes?'

'Ah well, there's always a risk about this sort of thing but I'm not really worried now. What worried me was when I came upon blocked places in that foul passage. I had to scratch and burrow like an old mole; the air was fetid at times—nothing but dust and mud. Still—I've

144

done it, and still live, thank God.'

I thanked God as well, in my heart.

'The trouble is,' he resumed, 'that old wreck won't help us any more. You may be sure the area will be well watched from now on.'

'A good thing too,' I said tartly, surprising even myself; I must have sounded exactly like Dame Jenny.

'And just what do you mean by that?' he asked in the hard determined way I knew so well.

I was confused and taken aback, realising I had actually no right to comment on what Mr Verne should or should not do.

My cheeks burned as I replied, 'I'm sorry, I suppose it isn't my place to speak like that. I was merely thinking of your safety. I mean—'

'Yes, do go on.'

'Well—you could—you could get seriously hurt or worse, couldn't you—if anything like this happened again? Have you *got* to go on with smuggling?'

He raised his brows and shrugged.

'A man like myself has to have certain things in his life such as—excitement of a kind perhaps—challenge, and the means of retaining certain standards, of having the luxuries he's used to.'

'Like your treasure room?'

His face was expressionless when he answered, 'Something of the sort.' It was as though a veil had clouded his features, and I knew he was thinking of the girl in the portrait. I was suddenly impatient, and filled with jealousy.

I went to the door abruptly, turned and said in matter-of-fact tones, 'You must be hungry. I know *I* am, after all the disturbance—'

'For which I profoundly apologise.' His voice was filled with mockery.

'There's cold ham,' I told him, ignoring the sarcasm. 'I'll make sandwiches and find something for Brutus. Come along, boy.'

Without waiting for Rupert's reply, I left the parlour, with the dog obediently at my heels.

Two o'clock struck when the snack meal I'd managed to provide was over. A curious silence had arisen between Rupert and me, an awkwardness filled with unspoken questions, doubts, hesitancy, and longings on my part, which made me gauche and unable to speak or behave naturally.

'You'll be very late back at Kerrysmoor, won't you?' I said at last. 'I mean, without a horse or anything—' I broke off stupidly. He got up from the chair, put a hand to the grazed cheek, which was no longer bleeding, and agreed with an ironic semblance of a short laugh. 'Certainly. My horse, I'm quite sure, is already back at the stables, in more respectable shape than I am. But a few miles' walk should freshen me up, and I know the quickest route there is.'

'Is it safe? Or would you rather—'

146

'Bide here till dawn?' The golden eyes gleamed with mockery. 'My dear girl! What man in his senses wouldn't? But under the circumstances it would be a little rash I think; in my own way I have principles, and I've no taste for testing them where you're concerned. A young woman of your type is—or *should* be—sacrosanct, in this particular instance. In other words—' His jaw tightened, the light in his eyes smouldered with the rising heat of desire, '—I *respect* you, Josephine, and if you go on looking at me like that, then heaven help both of us. I must be off, or dammit, darling, I'm only human—' He made a gesture of leaving, but I was before him at the door.

'No. Don't go.' The plea broke from me heedlessly. 'There's no need. I don't care a fig about respectability or what's done or not done. Rupert—please—'

He sighed, shaking his head slowly, then suddenly gave in, and gathered me to him, cradling my head against his breast. Half sobbing, half laughing with joy, I clung to him in complete abandonment, while he kissed my forehead, my cheeks and lips, burying his mouth in my hair. The scent and strength of his male body was all around—both a torment and opiate soothing and exciting me to forgetfulness of the world, of everything but the knowledge that it had happened at last. We were alone together, free to belong in the richest and deepest way possible to man and woman.

'Love me, Rupert,' I pleaded, as he carried me to the sofa, 'Oh, please, please love me.'

Very gently but firmly, he laid me down, and removed my wrap and nightshift. He was trembling. The scar near his shoulder showed briefly as he freed himself of constricting clothing. I touched it lightly, caressingly, but his lips were on mine again and the world was blotted out as our flesh became one, borne on a surging flood-tide of passion in which nothing registered but the wild fulfilment of mutual desire and need.

There was no doubting any more, no questioning or uncertainty. What had to be *was*, and had been destined assuredly as spring must follow winter, with summer's glory to follow.

When it was over we still lay entwined as emotional tumult died into sensuous sweet acceptance. My heart ached from an overburdening of joy. 'Until this moment,' I thought, 'I had no knowledge of what life could be. If I died now it would be with no regret, because heaven is here—beyond the limits of Time or mortality, and he is with me—'

'Darling—' I heard Rupert murmuring, stirring yet again closer. 'Oh, love, my love.' And like a flower suddenly brought to full blossoming, my body once more reached towards him, and was possessed, as was my

148

spirit, until peace came, and eventually we slept.

*   *   *

At the first streak of dawn before it was perfectly light, Rupert set off once more for Kerrysmoor, after a quick drink and a piece of cake I'd baked the previous day. He set off from the back of Tregonnis taking a short route I didn't know of, bordered by small stone-walled hills beneath the base of the moor. As his strong figure strode away to be lost in the half-light I wondered if Lady Verne would have missed his presence during the night, or even been aware of his absence. The mere thought of her existence momentarily chilled me. But when I went through to the kitchen doubt died in a rush of warm memory, and the knowledge that I was beloved.

All that morning I lived in a dream, untroubled by practical issues. It was only when evening approached that it occurred to me no concrete plan had been discussed concerning a future meeting. He would soon come, I knew that, but waiting was going to be a strain. I must be careful *always* of my appearance—never appear overtired or slipshod in the slightest way. My face must never be shiny from exertion or steamy from the washtub, nor my hair ungroomed. My aprons must be spotless, and my skin sweetly smelling

149

from cologne for his delight. There would be no difficulty in appearing the young lady of Tregonnis rather than its servant or caretaker, there was so little to do domestically without Dame Jenny. For myself I would keep cooking to a minimum, and prevail on Jan to spend more time washing the floors free of Brutus's footmarks and any mud stains brought in from his walks. I had made it my business to be friendly with the youth from the beginning of our acquaintanceship, and I think in an admiring fashion he liked me. He was also very loyal to Rupert.

So the first day passed, then another, and another.

Against my better judgement and optimism a niggle of anxiety seized me.

'Have you seen the master recently?' I asked Jan when the fifth afternoon arrived, and there was still no sign of Rupert.

He shook his head. 'I haven't seen en, Miss, he hasn' showed up at all when I took butter an' such to the big house. But I've heard tell 'er ladyship wasn' well, so I suppose he've bin spendin' more time with 'er. Nat'ral that, edn'et?'

'Oh yes, of course,' I replied mutely, thinking with an irrational burst of pain and disappointment, 'but it's not true. She may *call* herself his wife, but it's here he belongs—with *me* at Tregonnis.'

I longed to burst out with the truth. Let not

150

only Jan but the whole world know of our relationship. Love like ours should never be secret or hidden, but declared openly with honesty and pride.

Something of my inner struggle must have shown. 'Is everythin' all right, miss?' Jan asked. 'Nuthen wrong, is there?'

I pulled myself together quickly.

'No, nothing wrong at all,' I declared, hoping it was true. I was just wondering if—if her ladyship was likely to be ill for long.'

'Oh doan' worry 'bout 'er,' the boy said, with a laugh. 'She gets turns sometimes, an' then the Master has to be around, that's all.'

'What sort of turns?' I asked.

He shrugged, eyed me with curiosity for a moment, then replied, 'Just headaches. Megrims they call it at Kerrysmoor, the thing most fine high-up ladies suffer from, I do b'lieve.'

With that I had to be content; but fear, like a frail shadow, rose to haunt me, because I sensed more lay behind Jan's words than he was willing to admit, and that it very easily could concern me, and the night Rupert had spent at Tregonnis.

CHAPTER EIGHT

Another week passed following my conversation with Jan, before Rupert appeared.

It was a golden afternoon that day, and I was cutting a few of Dame Jenny's crimson roses for the boy to take to her when he went to Kerrysmoor the next morning. There was a slight breeze rippling the surface of the pool, and a sighing sound stirred the branches of an overhanging willow. Bees buzzed and a blackbird sang from a thorn tree. I was humming under my breath. That fact combined with Nature's murmuring was probably why I didn't at first hear footsteps approching along the path. The sound didn't properly register until he spoke.

'Josephine—'

I looked round sharply, and he was there, standing only a few yards away. At first I couldn't speak. Surprise, combined with a welling up of sudden joy shocked me to silence. Then I gave a little cry and ran to him. He kissed me. But the kiss was a gentle one. It was as though since our last passionate meeting something had happened that had drained energy and initiative from him. I stood back, studying him anxiously. His face too, appeared drawn. A little of the fire had left his eyes, but tenderness was there—a kind of weary compassion.

'What's wrong?' I asked. 'Is anything the matter?'

'My wife's—ill, as you must have heard or I should have been here earlier.'

'I'm sorry,' I said politely. 'Is her sickness serious?'

'Yes.'

'Are you trying to tell me we shan't—you won't be able to visit me or something?'

He moved towards me again; his touch on my shoulder felt for a brief moment like that of a parent trying to break bad news to a child. Instinctively I pulled myself away, and facing him with my chin raised an inch or two higher, said, 'Please don't try and evade the truth, Rupert. I'm a woman, and quite capable of hearing it. If you regret what happened, you've only got to say. But—'

In an instant his tired calm deserted him, and his arm was round me, while with the other hand he tilted my face up to his. This time his lips were firm and warm on mine. Through my thin dress I could feel the thudding of his heart. Then he released me, and I was thankful to see his countenance flooded with a warmer colour, and that something of the old flame lit his eyes.

'Don't you dare ever speak like that again,' he said sternly, 'or I'll have to spank sense into you. *Regret*! how can there be regret for the best thing that ever happened to me.'

'Then what *is* it?'

'For a time, my love, it's better for both of us that we don't meet too frequently. Only for a time, remember. After that—' he broke off hesitantly.

'Yes? Afterwards?'

'I think you know,' he replied ambiguously.

'I don't though,' I told him frankly. 'I *thought* I did—at least—perhaps I didn't think much about it—practically. But I *did* believe that in the end we'd be together.' I paused, continuing when he said nothing, 'Will we, Rupert?'

'My love, as soon as possible. In the meantime I'm quite sure you need something more to occupy you than being closeted alone here with only a great dog and occasional visit from Jan for company. So I've contacted my friend Luigi, and he's consented to give you further singing tuition, twice a week for so long as necessary to renew your confidence—'

I gasped.

'*Luigi*? But—I don't think I could. I don't *want* to any more. I simply couldn't face going through the kind of thing that happened at Exeter again. I know my voice is all right, of its kind—for singing at places like the Golden Bird. But not in opera. Truly, Rupert, fame isn't important to me any more. Surely you understand?'

'Yes, I understand what you feel at the moment; but Luigi still has great faith in your potential, so have I. You needn't necessarily make a career of your voice; that will be up to you; but the knowledge of being *able* to should count. Don't you understand, darling?'

I tried to, but it was difficult. Once more my life was in a whirl. From an over-quiet daily routine lit to expectancy each morning that the evening might possibly bring Rupert to my bed, I was suddenly confronted with a period of lessons under the tuition of the strict little Italian to whom I'd already brought disappointment and my own humiliation.

I protested strongly at first to Rupert's plan which meant that each Tuesday and Friday I would be taken to Truro in the chaise as before—and brought back again at a certain hour.

It was no use.

When I objected not only on personal grounds, but pointed out that the treasure room would be left unprotected, which was the primary reason that I'd stayed on following Dame Jenny's departure, he smiled reasoningly and assured me I needn't worry on such grounds. 'Beth Johns, a capable housemaid, will arrive with the chaise on the days of your departure,' he said, 'and be taken back again when you return. She's a sturdy character, quite capable of defending herself, if necessary, and she'll have Brutus don't forget.'

He paused. I was aggrieved, and when I didn't speak, he said, '*Please*, my love. For me.'

I wheeled round with a flurry of skirts and a flame of hot colour in my cheeks.

'Why for *you*? Is it your conscience pricking you or something? Why should my voice be suddenly so important again? Are you *frightened*, Rupert?'

His expression darkened. 'What the devil do you mean?' Both hands enclosed on my arms. I thought at first he was about to shake me, but he didn't.

I started at him defiantly and answered with a lurch of my heart, 'What I said— *frightened*—of her, your wife? Is *she* at the bottom of this?'

He freed me then, and his voice was cold when he replied, 'That is my business, Josephine. Some things must remain private to me—even from you.'

Misery engulfed me. 'Yes, yes—I'm sorry. Oh, Rupert—'

I turned away. The next moment I felt his mouth brush the nape of my neck at the back. His voice was soft against my ear when he murmured, 'Be patient. I love you. But unless you accept the situation as it is, it's just no good, Josephine. Remember I have other things in my life as well.'

Hope stirred in me.

'You mean the smuggling? But I thought—'

'What you thought is neither here nor there. Just trust me and be co-operative.' He swung me round. 'Is that understood?'

I sighed. 'All right. If you insist. But I can promise you I shan't enjoy it—having to tra-la and solfa before that fussy little man.'

'Oh I don't think it will be too bad,' he said ambiguously, obviously relieved. 'And now, look at me, you witch! and smile, d' you hear?'

I did; I couldn't help it. Against that certain warm look in his strange eyes I seemed to have no defence.

So the issue was settled, and the following week lessons recommenced with Signor Luigi in Truro.

They weren't so onerous as I'd expected. He was unexpectedly pleasant to me, and assured me he'd never lost interest or faith in my voice.

'Your patron though—my good friend, Mr Verne—has slightly different plans for its promotion,' he said affably, 'or shall we say its use.'

'Oh?'

'Opera, he told me, is not entirely to your fancy, at the moment, so we shall take a lighter approach in training—calculated for a more suitable role such as highly born ladies indulge in, at soirees and in drawing rooms.'

'*Drawing* rooms?' I gasped.

He smiled, stroking his little beard, with a calculating look in his bright eyes. 'You have all the potential it takes to become the rage and toast—the reigning queen of fashionable gatherings,' he stated. 'That is the line we shall follow from now on. Movements and grace

157

will also play an important part. I can assure you when your coaching is completed, no duchess in the land will compare.'

'But I don't *want* to be a duchess, or a—a warbling socialite creature,' I exclaimed rashly. 'I'm not like that. I'm *me*—Josephine Lebrun. Rupert—I mean Mr Verne—is *wrong* in trying to make me into something different. Oh I don't think having lessons again is a good idea at all.'

'Maybe not at the moment,' the little man said acerbically, 'but you *will*. It's what you're here for, and I trust you're not going to be difficult. Under the circumstances such an attitude would be most unfair—to me.'

Realising there was no point in arguing I gave in with as good a grace as possible and decided piquantly that if I was destined to become a drawingroom party-piece and dainty triller of ballads, then I should dress in a manner befitting the character. I would write a note to Rupert telling him my wardrobe needed refurbishing, had I his permission to order a new cloak and bonnet, and if it was not asking too much two new gowns also from the costumier's in Truro, as I did not now care to appear in Signor Luigi's presence dressed in anything but the best. Yes, I would do that, and send the note by Jan, or the coachman. Either Rupert would have to reply, or call in person at Tregonnis to give an answer. The mischievous impulse stimulated and lifted my spirits considerably, and after making the decision I had the note ready for the man to take on the next day when I returned by chaise from Truro.

The following morning Jan was due to call at Kerrysmoor with some farm produce, and I waited hopefully for his return, and a message. It was twelve o'clock before the youth got back.

'The Master sent this for you,' he said, handing me a gilt-edged envelope. 'Tell Miss Lebrun to give et to the place marked in Truro, and everythin' should be all right, he said.'

'Very well, thank you, Jan.'

When he'd gone I looked at the name on the envelope. It was addressed to the most select costumiers in the City, and was unsealed. So obviously I had permission to read what was inside:

Madam, I should be obliged if you would equip Miss Josephine Lebrun with any select feminine garments she fancies. I am sure your advice would be of great help to her as she is likely to be launched socially at a suitable time in the future. Expense in this case is of no consideration. If you let me know what is owed I will see you have the sum at the nearest possible date.

Yours truly,

Rupert Verne.

'Launched into society,' I thought. How very ridiculous when at the moment all that Rupert appeared to wish—except for my sessions with Luigi—was to keep me pushed away at Tregonnis. Still, I would certainly take advantage of his offer and acquire the most elegant and flattering gowns in the fashionable establishment—if only for *his* benefit, so that his desire would be intensified and he would be stimulated somehow to decide what future we could have together.

Madame Juliette's salon was situated in the vicinity of Lemon Street. It was richly carpeted, with tall mirrors placed conveniently at every angle for viewing the figure, and curtained wardrobes intriguingly parted to display clothing of a tempting variety—luxurious more than of a utility type. Flowery and be-feathered headgear rested daintily on tall stands; gilt furniture of a French style was arranged so that it allowed a wide space for clients to wander to and fro studying their reflections under cunningly contrived lighting. Tall-stemmed flowers in crystal vases added an exotic, yet delicate, atmosphere and the air was fragrant with subtle perfume. Everything, in fact, induced an expensive sense of luxury that was both stimulating and relaxing.

Feeling free to choose, and mildly mischievous, I wandered about for some time trying this and that, while Madame Juliette obsequiously 'modomed' and flattered me. As time passed a faint irritation sounded in her voice. I wasn't surprised—no high-born lady in the land could have appeared more demanding and critical than the creature I was pretending to be for that intriguing half-hour.

However, at last my choice was made: a deep lilac satin gown, having an over-mantle of olive green velvet trimmed with violet braid; and a cream heavy silk costume consisting of a short-waisted coatee and full skirt gathered from the hips to the back forming the suggestion of a bustle. The hem of the skirt was heavily embroidered in gold thread, and there were tiny gold buttons down the front of the coat. To go with it I discovered a cream boat-shaped hat to be worn saucily tilted forward; it was trimmed with osprey and had chiffon veiling behind.

Then there were accessories of fine kid gloves, and a feather boa—a gilt chain handbag also, and cream boots with pointed toes. Oh, I was very rash, stimulated not only by vanity but a touch of defiance to make Rupert once more aware of my presence in his life. I doubted that he could grudge the expense, although I was sure that her ladyship would, if she ever found out.

Lady Verne!

As usual, whenever the thought of her crossed my mind a vague shadow of resentment fell on me. Rupert might not love her—I was sure he didn't. But she was always

161

there, in the background, his wife, and therefore the one with legal power. There were two of them really who stood as obstacles to my love, I thought that day when I left Madame Juliette's: Lady Alicia, and that girl in the portrait, the elusive beauty whose claim at Tregonnis remained a mystery, and haunted my imagination every time I caught her wistful stare from its heavy frame.

Two days following my second new singing session with Signor Luigi, Rupert called to tell me that my famous tutor was pleased with my voice and my acceptance of his new plans for me. The girl from Kerrysmoor who came for a few hours daily, had already left and I was chagrined that I was not wearing one of my new gowns for his attention.

'You mean *your* new plans,' I corrected him.

'Ah well! let us say *mutual*,' he agreed, smiling. 'You should be pleased—it's a guarantee, isn't it, that I intend our life together to be far closer after certain obstacles have been worked out.' He took my hand, drew me close and embraced me warmly.

'It would be more helpful if you could tell me how—explain just a little,' I pointed out. 'Signor Luigi speaks a lot about drawingrooms and social occasions, but I'm not really a drawingroom kind of person. Is that what *you're* looking for? Someone to entertain at your grand parties warbling away while some stuffy accompanist pounds ballads on a piano.

Is that what *she* was—the girl in the portrait?'

The moment the question was out I could have cut my tongue out. Rupert's face darkened. In a strange way it seemed to close up—shutting me out. 'I'm sorry,' I added quickly, 'I didn't mean to—to pry, but—'

'You're too curious by half,' he said shortly, 'and I don't like it. Impertinence, even from you, is extremely distasteful. Remember that in the future, Josephine. When I wish to confide in you I will. Do you understand?'

'Very well,' I said. 'I'm sorry.'

He softened a little. 'Forget it. You're very young still, and have a lot to learn. Maybe—' he shrugged, '—we both have. It's so long since—' He broke off aggravatingly and made to leave. 'Well, I must be off now, I've much to do. Take care of yourself—I felt I had to drop in and tell you how pleased I was about the lessons, and also, by the way, that you'd assembled a new wardrobe in Truro.'

He kissed me before he left. But more gently than usual; it was as though his mind was on other things. A little disappointed I turned away and went through the kitchen into the garden. The clippety-clop of his horse's hooves gradually died away into the distance. I felt alone, and resentful of the secret places in his heart and life that I could not share.

Sunlight was only fitful that day, but towards evening the clouds broke up leaving clear skies lit with dying gold over the moors.

163

My spirits lifted. I would have gone for a stroll, but Jan had taken Brutus for a 'good ole gallop' as he put it, because the dog had been left on his own a good deal lately, and needed 'a bit o' fun like'.

The air was heady with the scents and soft murmurings of summertime. I walked down the garden path to the wilderness covering the passage used by Rupert on the night of his escape from the Revenue. Once more the weeds and briars had crawled across the entrance leaving only a glimmer of darkness through the tangled branches. I returned to the site of Dame Jenny's roses and broke one idly from its stem, holding it to my nose and drawing the sweetness into my lungs. Then I wandered to the pool, thinking dreamily and longingly of the treasured hours when Rupert and I had lain and loved together through that never-to-be-forgotten night.

Frail reflections and shadows of early evening already patterned the surface of the water. A kind of enchantment enfolded me, inducing me to sing in a low tone—a sweet-sad melody in a minor key that I'd heard in far-away childhood. I was aware of no other sound—of no other human being invading the solitude, so my senses froze when a ripple of strange laughter broke the peace. The song died on my lips.

At the same moment, as I started to turn my head, the touch of hands brushed the back of my neck, gradually tightening until I could hardly breathe. At first I didn't attempt to move, sensing that my resistance might mean danger. Then there was a further laugh, deeper this time, holding a subtle obscene triumph. I managed to strain round briefly to catch a glimpse of the intruder. What I saw shocked me—a pale malicious face staring from glassy mad eyes. A trickle of saliva coursed down the long chin from twisted lips.

I was terrified. The grip on my body seemed to have super-human strength.

'Don't move,' whispered a thick harsh voice, while thumbs pressed deeper into my neck. 'Like the other one, aren't you? Trollop— staring down from her great frame. And where did it get her—*where*—?' The voice became a hiss. 'In the pool. Drowned like a rat.'

I was propelled round and pushed forwards so I thought I must surely tumble in. But the hard arms still held me. Shadows drifted and faded in the cool water. 'There she is—*there!*' the malignant tones continued. 'Watch her eyes where the fish swim. Holes now in an empty skull. And she was his once—his dream. He loved her. *Love!*' Wild laughter momentarily shrieked through the air. 'And she still is. So—leave here you fool—or you'll end up like her and the Three Maidens. The Three Maidens, do you *hear*?' I was shaken wildly and forced to face the creature again.

There was no smile now on the macabre lips.

Only hate.

Then suddenly it was as though all force left the wild figure. The arms dropped from my shoulder and neck, and like some grotesque great bird from a nightmare, the shape in its black cloak turned and fled flapping crazily to the lane where it disappeared into the shadow of the trees. I sank on to the ground with my head bowed to ward off faintness. How long I stayed there I don't know. But presently I heard Jan's whistle from the fields followed by the happy barking of a dog. The youth and Brutus appeared minutes later. By then I had got up and was already in the kitchen.

'Why, missie,' the youth said, after one glance at my face, 'Whatever's the matter with ee? Anythin' wrong? You do look frit to death—'

I tried to speak, but it was difficult to be coherent. My throat hurt so. 'Someone— attacked me,' I managed to say at last. 'It was—I don't know—who. You'd better tell the Master—'

'But I can't do that, Miss Jo—I've heard tell he took himself off on business 'bout an hour 'go—Truro or somewhere, maybe Plymouth, I doan' know. But I could get a message to her ladyship—'

I lifted a hand in negation. '*No.*' Even in my own ears my voice was a mere rasp. 'Don't tell her, whatever you do. It's all right—' I swallowed painfully. 'I've Brutus now. And—

and the girl comes in the morning.'

He looked dubious. 'Ef the Master did know he'd get the p'lice mebbe—'

I shook my head. 'It's all over now. With the dog and the doors locked there'll be no danger. I shall—I shall be all right.'

He looked doubtful but in the end agreed. 'S'long as you keep Brutus with ee when th' girl edn' here,' he said. 'It's my fault p'raps f'r leavin' y' alone—although it wasn' f'r long. But if Master Verne knew, I'd get the push from Farmer Carne sure 'nuff.'

I managed to smile.

'Farmer Carne *won't* know,' I promised, 'and neither will Master Verne. You're a good lad, Jan, I wouldn't want to get you into trouble.' He scratched one ear thoughtfully. 'Thank 'ee, Miss. I hope I'm doin' right.'

'I'm sure you are. And it's best not to worry the Master anyway.'

'Yes. That's right. He does have plenty to worry him without any more shoved on him. I'll say goodnight to ee then.' And still shaking his head thoughtfully he left Tregonnis for the farm.

Later I wondered what his reference to Rupert's worries meant. But I was still too bewildered and upset to think clearly. I had Brutus sleeping by my bed that night, with the pistol on my side table, but it was a long time before I got any rest. I recalled the harsh voice's reference to 'the Three Maidens', and to the girl in the portrait, and when at last I slept my dreams were of a witch-like face glaring down on me, and of a fair face upturned—a floating image in the pool—the face of the girl in the portrait.

When I woke in the morning my neck was still swollen. The next day I was due for my lesson with Signor Luigi, but I knew there would be no point in going to Truro. Although I could speak, somewhat gruffly, I couldn't sing. When I tried nothing came from my throat but a rasping cough. My voice had gone. How permanently I didn't know. It was a terrible feeling thinking I might never sing again.

CHAPTER NINE

For the next few days following the assault my neck was still swollen, and dark bruises showed at the throat. None of my dresses could be buttoned near the chin, so I swathed chiffon round the neck to hide the marks, fastened with a cameo brooch. The effect was not perfect, but to any casual observer would give, hopefully, no sign of injury. To the daily girl I simply made excuses of having caught 'some kind of a cold in my throat' and Jan did not give me away. When the chaise arrived to take me to Truro I asked the man if he would be kind enough to drive there and inform the maestro that I was unwell and not likely to be able to attend the theatre for a little while. At the same time I concocted an excuse for needing cough mixture from the apothecary's and told the man I'd be grateful if the mixture could be picked up and delivered to me at Tregonnis.

The coachman was dubious at first, but when I asked if Mr Verne was back at Kerrysmoor, if so I was sure he would give permission, I was told no, the Master was still away, having had to take a trip to Plymouth.

'And her ladyship?' I questioned, although the girl had already informed me she was in a mood.

He shook his head. 'She still isn't well, Miss.'

'Then *please*—my voice is so rough, and I can hardly swallow—'

Eventually the man agreed.

When the sound of horses' hooves and wheels rattling down the road had died away, I went back into the house, miserably wondering if the Plymouth business had anything to do with Rupert's contraband interests. Even with the girl and Brutus for company I was miserable and on edge, and still very shocked. At night I locked and bolted the doors early, and left Brutus free to roam the cottage— except for the Treasure Room, for fear his animal presence might dislodge any precious relic.

I slept badly; but one evening, about five days following the attack at the pool I was so exhausted I went upstairs early, and immediately on getting into bed fell into a heavy sleep.

It must have been about two o'clock when I woke suddenly, disturbed by a sound below—a crashing noise followed by a tinkle and several short bangs. I felt my whole body go rigid except for the wild thumping of my heart. For some moments I lay unmoving, waiting for Brutus's heavy snarl and growling.

There was nothing.

Everything, after a matter of only minutes, was completely deadly quite. Had I been dreaming, I asked myself, and woken from some nightmare? Or was I perhaps no longer completely sane and balanced following my frightening experience? I knew somehow I had to pull myself together and venture downstairs to find out what had happened, and if Brutus was all right. So I pulled on a wrap and slippers, crept out of the bedroom and tip-toed to the top of the stairs. I paused, then, listening.

'Brutus,' I called in a croaky whisper, '—Brutus, Brutus—'

There was no response.

Cautiously I went down.

The dog was lying completely still, as though unconscious or dead, near the front door; there was blood and a small amount of red meat lying nearby, and the pane of a small side

170

window had been carefully cut away. I caught my breath with horror and rushed to the dog's side. He was still breathing, and appeared not to have been hurt, but a curious smell came from the meat. Obviously he had been poisoned in some way, or drugged.

Jan, I thought, I must get Jan. But at such an hour it would mean walking a distance to the farm and then rousing the whole household. In the meantime further vandalism might occur. I was still wondering what to do, when the animal stirred; one eye opened, then another. There was a feeble wag of the tail, and with relief I realised the dog was recovering. It was then I noticed the door of the Treasure Room. The lock had been somehow forced, and it was half open. Holding my candle shakily, I went in.

Glass lay shattered everywhere about the floor, with one or two figurines; but that was all. Torn from its frame and ripped into several pieces was the portrait of the girl. The lovely limpid eyes stared up at me through the wan flickering light. Her head was severed from the body at the throat, and by it was a piece of cardboard on which, scrawled in wild zig-zaggy writing, were the words: 'THE THREE MAIDENS. Now there are *Four*'.

A fit of trembling shook me from head to foot. Whoever had committed the destruction could be no other, I was sure, than the mad creature who'd assaulted me in the garden. But

171

why? And *how* had Brutus been kept quiet then drugged, while the break-in was made? He was a trained guard, only obeying a well-known voice. Then it must be someone at Kerrysmoor. And that someone must be Lady Verne! Was it possible? She disliked me, yes. But she was ill, bedridden, and the malicious damage had been directed more towards the portrait than myself—except for the garden episode, and I certainly had not recognised her ladyship in the attacker.

Somehow I got through the morning. The loneliness was frightening—intense, and Jan did not call at the usual hour to take the dog for his walk. No one came—no one, until early in the afternoon when a handy-man from Kerrysmoor arrived on a horse with a message to say the girl who usually helped at Tregonnis on certain days was unavailable, and that under the circumstances, Master Verne thought it better for me to go to Truro for a few days. A room had been booked for me at The Crown coaching house, he'd be in touch with me sometime, there. The chaise would pick me up at four o'clock.

'I don't understand,' I said in my rusty voice. 'I have a cold in my throat, and—and why must I leave here so quickly?—Who'll look after the cottage?' My objection of course was quite stupid. I should have been grateful for the chance of avoiding another night alone at Tregonnis.

172

'That'll be all looked after, Miss,' the man said. 'There's a note here from Mr Verne. He's got back not long since. Perhaps you'd better read it.'

I took the envelope from him and tore it open:

Josephine, please do what I wish—pack a few things and be ready for the chaise to pick you up by four. Things are happening here which are exceedingly unpleasant. I have sent instructions to The Crown to see that you are comfortably accommodated. I shall see you as soon as possible. When that will be I cannot say. Until then, yours as ever, Rupert.

I looked up at the man, bewildered, shocked, and taken aback by the brevity of the note which seemed to imply great anxiety on his part to get me out of the way—or was it out of his life?

'Why didn't Mr Verne come himself?' I asked. 'And does he—do *any* of you up at Kerrysmoor know what's been happening *here*? But of course not. How could you—?' I broke off coughing.

We were standing at the gate of the garden. The man was holding his horse by the bridle, and the animal whinnied shrilly, as though sensing my distress.

'Is something wrong, Miss?'

I gave the semblance of a laugh, a derisive gruff sound.

'You'd better come and have a look.'

He tethered his mount to a sycamore, and followed me up the path into the house.

'Sakes almighty,' he exclaimed, 'how did this happen?'

'Last night—about two o'clock,' I explained. 'I was in bed and was woken up by a sound. No—not Brutus. *He* was—he must have been drugged. I came downstairs and found—*this*.'

The man simply gaped, patting the dog's head idly, as it gazed up at him mournfully, wagging his tail in a lazy way. 'He seems all right now,' he said at length. 'And that's something.'

'Oh yes, Brutus will soon be his old self I'm sure. But don't you think you should inform your Master what has occurred as soon as possible and have investigations started? The vet too. The vet should have a look at Brutus.'

'Yes, yes. Of course. I'll be gone, and you may be sure someone'll be around—the police most likely to take charge of things. I can tell Master Verne you'll be ready then to go to Truro as he said?'

I nodded bleakly, and without further ado the man left kicking his mount to a swift pace down the lane, towards the main road.

In a daze I went upstairs to my bedroom and began mechanically to pack my small valise,

174

feeling in an unreal dream that had the quality of an unending nightmare. I put a cape and bonnet ready on the bed, and when I looked at the clock saw I had an hour and a half to wait. But before then, I told myself, someone would arrive—Rupert? Oh surely, Rupert himself must come when he learned what a terrifying experience I'd been through.

Waiting can be agonising. From time to time I wandered through the cottage aimlessly, tidying this and that, talking to Brutus who seemed content to rest in the hall—thinking as each quarter of an hour passed, 'Why doesn't he come, or at least send *someone*? A fast horse has had plenty of time—? Suppose some lurking madman or murderer appears again suddenly? All I have is Brutus who's still shocked, and the gun—the pistol. Where is it?' I searched my mind wildly for a moment, then remembered it was in a drawer in my bedroom. I went upstairs again, found it, and put it in a pocket of my gown. Then I returned to the parlour.

When, at half past three still no one had arrived, nervous exhaustion drove me to a quick decision. I would wait no longer. I *couldn't*. If Rupert cared for me at all—and I'd believed in him so deeply, so truly—he'd somehow have contrived to rescue me before this from Tregonnis, which had now become no more than a sinister prison. But he didn't love me. He never had—not sufficiently anyway. Whatever it was that was keeping us apart at such a dangerous time—whether some smuggling business, or her ladyship's 'me-grims' (what a word, I thought contempt-uously) any feeling he had for me was of merely secondary consideration to him. And I knew I could no longer bear it. I didn't want his charity, his help, or being pushed about from one place to another without any explanation, just because it suited him. I didn't want any drive to Truro in his rich chaise just to be closeted in some stuffy hostelry at his command. If I hadn't a real place in his heart, I wanted nothing of him at all. For a time he'd desired me—and managed to win me. But now it seemed it was over; he was being devious and polite, and maybe in his way trying to fit me into some kind of mutual future. On the other hand, perhaps not.

Either way it didn't matter. I was weary of fretting, and hoping and fighting the long terrifying hours without him.

I would make a clean break. I could still do it—I was young and strong, and one day, surely, when the bruises in my neck faded and healed, my voice would return. So I'd leave on my own and somehow make my way back to Falmouth. Taking a route along the coastal lanes below the moors I could be there, walking, in a matter of two days, perhaps even less. Furthermore, if I hurried, I could catch a private waggon that drove part of the way, leaving Tharne each evening at four-thirty. So I'd hurry, and start off immediately for the village before Rupert's chaise arrived.

Once my plan was made I allowed no other consideration to change it. The past was over and a new period in my life beginning. I must somehow forget Rupert—or at least blot him from my mind.

In this hard determined mood it was that some time later I was ensconced in Mr Jago's private waggon, with five other passengers jolting along the road southwards towards Falmouth. After numerous stopping places I left the vehicle at Penhallow and from there started walking cross country, avoiding Redlake, in the direction of my home town.

* * *

The air was sweet with the tang of heather, thyme, gorse, and a salty mild wind blown from the sea. I wore my lightest boots, and loosened my cape at the neck. Gulls occasionally wheeled overhead, and everywhere were the low rustling sounds of Nature's creatures about their secret ways.

Sometimes I left the lanes for farm footpaths, but mostly I kept to narrow roadways used from hamlet to hamlet, and frequented I supposed chiefly by gypsies, pedlars, or wanderers like myself wishing to avoid attention. As I had money in my reticule it was easy enough to call at a wayside tavern or cottage and find temporary resting place and something to eat. Directions of route were willingly provided, 'always bear left now,' I was told at one small kiddleywink, 'keepin' that theer old mine Wheal Flower on th' right. An' kip thy face an' gold hid, case some lurkin' vag'bond spies 'ee.'

I took the advice for some part of the way after leaving, but as the lane climbed upwards and vegetation became more sparse giving a clear view on every side, I removed the hood of my cape from my face, and let the fresh air brush my cheeks and loosen my hair. A pedlar passed driving a cart pulled by an old donkey; pots and pans rattled, together with the sound of creaking cart wheels. The man was a wizened, puckish-looking fellow, with a blue feather in his hat. The vehicle was loaded with a conglomeration of goods—bottles of lotions, ribbons, winking glass beads, cutlery, household goods, and haberdashery of all sorts, mostly secondhand, I guessed. He drew up the cart and introduced himself as Barnaby Goine.

'Give 'ee a lift, missus?' he asked with a lopsided grin showing a single broken tooth. 'Or wantin' a pretty ring are 'ee?—or mebbee a ribbon for thy pretty hair?'

I declined the offer of a lift, there appeared to be no room anyway, but bought a glass bauble I didn't want just to show goodwill, and presently with a word in the old nag's ear he was away again, and I continued walking, keeping always slightly to my left.

The sky began to fade into twilight and bringing a greenish glow to the landscape. As the stark dark shape of Wheal Flower faded ever further behind me, I began to feel tired. How many miles I'd walked since leaving Mr Jago's waggon, I didn't know. But at last, to my relief, from a high point of the lane I saw far ahead of me and below, the darkening silhouettes of buildings against the paler glimmer of sea, and knew I was approaching Falmouth.

I arrived, heavy-limbed from carrying my valise, about an hour later. Lights dotted the streets and waterside, and a lump of emotion seized me, whether for good or ill, no one could say.

I had come home.

Wearily I threaded my way down narrow cobbled byways leading to the harbour. I must have looked a sight indeed, when I reached The Golden Bird. But the landlord, astounded at first, welcomed me.

'So it's you,' he said, as I tried vainly to adjust my bonnet, 'Come in, my dear, come in. This place hasn't been the same since you left.' He took my case, and shouted for his wife. 'She's back, luv, our nightingale's back with us.'

He didn't know then that I couldn't sing.

CHAPTER TEN

Joe Burns and his wife, Maria, were heavily disappointed when I had to admit to them then my voice had gone. I invented a story that I'd been involved in a carriage accident, hence the scars on my neck, but that shock as well contributed to my sorry state. News travels quickly, and I didn't wish Rupert to hear in some roundabout way what had happened, or even, at the moment, of my whereabouts.

'I shall recover in time, I'm sure,' I told them, with more optimism than I felt. 'In the meantime, if I can stay here for a bit, I'd be very grateful. I have money. I can pay—'

'There's no need for payment—' Joe said quickly, but his wife interrupted, 'Now wait a bit, Joe. If Josie's got it to spare—only a *very* little mind you, just a token as they say—she'd probably rather. She was always the independent sort, weren't you, love?'

'Yes,' I agreed honestly. 'I would rather give something.'

'Only until it's convenient to you then,' Joe agreed grudgingly, 'and when you c'n sing again the boot'll be on the other foot. There'll be a good salary coming along.'

So a minimum weekly sum was arranged. I had sufficient in my pocket to cover at least a month, or two. And when that was gone? If my

180

voice never properly came back again? The thought was frightening. I knew the Burnses would never turn me adrift, but I wanted to feel secure in some way, to depend entirely on *no-one*—neither Joe, Maria, nor—Rupert.

Should I ever see him again? If he really wanted to find me would he recall the Golden Bird and walk in one night as he had the first time I ever saw him, tall hat in hand, his yellow eyes searching through the crowds and lamplight for a sight of me? I was pondering the question to myself when Maria put a suggestion to me one evening.

'You haven't told us the whole story, have you, girl?' she asked. 'About your singing, and what happened between you and that fine gentleman, Mr Verne—'

'I—'

She lifted a hand. 'No. I don't want to pry, but it seems to me not natural you should just be staying in the background all the time, or taking a walk round the streets when there's life here you could enjoy. After all singing isn't everything. You've still got your looks, and your legs is all right, aren't they?'

I gave a short laugh.

'My legs? Why—yes, I suppose so. They weren't broken or anything. But what makes you ask?'

She shrugged.

'You c'n dance as well as sing. There's a man, Johnny Bliss, that comes here every night now. Plays the fiddle real good. A smart one, Johnny. Been on the sea and lost a leg in a shindig with pirates. He'd play for you an' make a handsome turn of it. Why don't you try, girl? You're fretting 'bout something, and that's no good for the young. Joe'd pay you too, an' don't say you carry the wealth o' the world in your pocket. You dropped your reticule in the bedroom the other afternoon when you went wandering, and it'd spilled over the floor. I picked it up for 'ee. Not much there, Josie—well, you just think about it.'

I did, and although the prospect didn't appeal to me at first, after my first negative reaction I began to see possibilities. Perhaps at the back of my mind, too, was the sneaking idea that such a plan might enable Rupert and me to meet again.

'But I've no dancing clothes with me now,' I told Maria when she next broached the matter. 'I've only the clothes I came in, a few undergarments and a spare dress—it's much too sophisticated.'

'H'm. Yes. You're certainly quite a young madam to look at these days,' Maria said thoughtfully. 'But I've a Japanese shawl tucked away upstairs, and when you went there were slippers left behind, and a flowery skirt. They earrings, and a few flash beads—oh, we could fit you up all right.'

Eventually I agreed, and when I tried the bright garments on the following afternoon a little of the lost magic of former days returned. I longed and longed to sing as well as pirouetting only to Johnny Bliss's fiddle, but my voice, though clear enough by then for talking, was just a harsh croak when I attempted any melody. I found Johnny amusing. He was a wiry ginger-haired little man, half Cornish, half Irish, with a whimsical one-sided smile, and bright eyes filled with mischievous humour.

An hour before the bar opened we had, as he called it, 'a try-out', and for the first time in months I felt an uplift of spirits. There was no command to move gracefully or with dignity—no sharp reminder that I must control myself as befitting the part I was playing—no—'Now return and make your entrance again' as there'd been time after time at Signor Luigi's. I was free—*free* to sway and gesture and kick my heels uninhibited by restrictions or etiquette. With my hair loose, and to Johnny's winks and elfin manner of playing and half dancing, I could be for however brief a time, myself. And it was invigorating.

Joe and Maria watching the rehearsal, were delighted. 'You must come on tonight, girl,' Joe said. 'Word will soon get around then. We'll be the best known tavern in all Falmouth.'

And so it was.

Keeping my thoughts firmly away from

Rupert or Tregonnis, I was able to put all my conscious capacity for life and enjoyment into dancing. I became, as days passed, a popular feature at the inn, and by degrees even the lingering hope and possibility that Rupert might appear one night, died into a mere shadow.

Then, one evening, at the very end of the performance I felt suddenly faint. No one noticed—not even Maria, who was helping Joe at the bar. I managed to retire after blowing a kiss to the blurred faces crowding the tap room, and somehow made my way upstairs. Once there I lay on my bed and waited for the unpleasant feeling to pass. My face and hands were dripping by then with cold sweat, and there was a sickening pain under the pressure of my corsets. Presently I felt better, but by then a suspicion was growing in my mind that I'd never even considered before.

Suppose I was with child?

Could it possibly be? But of course it could. When two people loved—or *had* loved as Rupert and I had—any sensible person would know better than to be shocked by the suggestion.

Elation, mingled with fear and a sense of unreality seized me. I couldn't visualise the future. I didn't try.

But that night I had a dream.

I was standing on a lonely hill—black as a moonless night under a cold sky. There was no wind, no sound at all; the air was icy cold—the ground hard and lifeless like that of a dead land. I tried to move, but at first my limbs were fixed and motionless; then slowly my head lifted, and the summit of the hill clarified into the shapes of three grotesque hooded figures, who slowly, menacingly, dragged themselves from the earth towards me.

Magnetised by horror, my unwilling feet moved upwards. Black arms, like the wings of great crows reached to the sky, then slowly, rhythmically descended, gaunt clawlike hands gropingly thrust to my neck. I caught a glimpse of hungry ravaged faces with twisted lips—teeth bared, approaching in a strange haunted rhythm. And in a flash recognition swept through me in blinding terror.

Lady Verne!—Lady Verne!

For a second I was rooted again to the foul earth. It seemed as though my feet were sucked into a sickening mire of evil. Then, suddenly, sight failed. I tottered backwards and fell—fell into the well of darkness swirling round me in a suffocating cloud.

I screamed then, screamed and screamed, until no longer even sound registered. I knew no more until I woke up, bathed in perspiration, with my heart pounding heavily against my ribs, and my whole body shaking.

As surroundings of my room at the inn came into focus, the door opened and Maria entered, her face full of concern in the flickering light of the candle.

'Sakes alive!' she exclaimed. 'Whatever's the matter, girl? Enough to waken the dead it was—that *noise!*—thought you were being murdered for sure. What was it, girl? What's the matter?' she bent down, studying me anxiously.

'I had a nightmare,' I answered. 'A dream. It was awful. I'm so sorry.'

She went to the ewer, poured some water into the basin, and returned with a cloth to wipe my forehead. 'There, there,' she murmured soothingly, 'You'll be all right presently. Just take it easy. Something you had to eat, maybe?'

I shook my head. 'It was the Three Maidens and her—her. It was—' I broke off, knowing the fear was still on me, and that in any case Maria wouldn't know what I was talking about—I hardly knew myself.

'Three maidens? Who are they then? Now you tell me what it's all about. Seems to me you've bin seein' strange sights since you went off with that fine gentleman. I never did approve of it in the first place, and I said so to Joe. *Italians!*' she gave a sceptical short laugh. 'You wasn't bred for furriners and their carryings on, girl. Now you just rest quiet, and there'll be no more dancing, and remembering wicked goings on. If you're no better later I'll have the apothecary to see you.'

My head ached badly all day, and when

night came I had a fever. Dr Prynne, Solomon Prynne, who was not only regarded as a fine medical man, but a clever 'wizard' as well, came to examine me and provided some pills and herbal remedies which he said would be of great assistance in easing the pain.

'Then, later, we shall have to see,' he said, rubbing his chin thoughtfully, and I started to laugh, thinking how much like a goat he looked, with his wispy beard and tufts of hair sticking upwards on either side of his wide forehead.

Maria looked at me aghast. 'It isn't funny, Josie,' she said. 'Dr Prynne's doing his best to help you. What the joke is I cannot for the life of me see.'

'No—no,' I apologised weakly. 'I'm sorry.'

The 'goat' patted my hand reassuringly, took a small glass from his case, poured something into it from a bottle, and bid me take it. I swallowed it chokingly, not caring at the moment what it did to me—whether I lived or died seemed suddenly quite unimportant.

Minutes later the two of them walked quietly from the room, Dr Prynne's boots making a squeaky creaking sound, just like the whinnying of the goat he so resembled.

On such a thought my senses began to relax, taking fear with it, until I drifted into peaceful slumber.

How long I slept I didn't realise. At times I roused, and recalled being fed from a spoon and given more of the pills and draught. Days must have passed in this semi-conscious state, or maybe weeks, I had no manner of judging. But one morning, magically, I felt better.

I remembered everything. Not all at once, but piece by piece, putting facts together like the pieces of a puzzle.

'How long have I been ill?' I asked Maria when she came in with my morning gruel.

'A week or two, but you're better now. Oh how pleased Joe will be too. It's been worrying for us, girl. But Dr Prynne—he said you'd be all right in the end. Some sort of shock, he said, and then that strange fever following! Later you'll have to tell us properly what's been happening. It's only fair, love.'

'Yes. Yes, I know. But—'

'Not yet. Oh, there's no hurry. You just take things easy and do a bit each day—not much mind you, but—'

'I've got money,' I said, as I'd told her before. 'Not a lot, I suppose, perhaps not sufficient to repay what you've done for me. But I can work, can't I?—I could help in the taproom perhaps—the bar; if I don't—'

'Tut-tut!' she exclaimed, 'no more silly talk. You're our nightingale—our own Golden Bird whether you c'n sing or not. Tomorrow's tomorrow, remember, and today's today. So we'll remember that shall we, and just get on with the present.'

And that is just what we did. By the time I'd

recovered sufficiently to take proper walks about the harbour and help Joe and Maria run the inn, autumn was already turning the leaves of the trees to yellow, and evenings closed in bringing salty grey mists from the sea. I neither saw nor heard anything of Rupert, but one day, overcome by the sudden nauseous feeling for no reason whatever—or so I thought—a very tangible fact registered that was bound to affect my whole life.

What I'd guessed before was true.

I was going to have a child.

*   *   *

For two months I waited, saying nothing to anyone about my condition, being careful to hide any fits of nausea I felt, and not worrying unduly about the future; indeed, a strange kind of placidity enveloped me. Whatever trials, challenges, and maybe disappointment in life awaited me, at least my love for Rupert had not been entirely in vain; something of him already thrived within me—something no one could take away. Even my sleep became comparatively peaceful. Following the horror of the dreadful nightmare the scene changed. In my dreams I wandered through an unreal but generally pleasant vista of meadowlands and ethereal waving grasses, with a young boy, a child, holding my hand. When I woke I never recalled his face clearly, and seldom felt any fear or real anxiety, although just occasionally a sadness lingered, like the sadness of trying to recapture an old forgotten tune.

'That rich Mr Verne you used to know—' Joe said to me one day, 'they say he's not there any more—'

My heart jerked for a second, stood still, and then raced on again. 'Gone away, do you mean?' I asked.

'Not exactly. But I've heard tell he goes up country a lot. Funny though—he called the other day—'

'Here? At the Golden Bird?' I gasped.

'That's right,' Joe answered, polishing a glass and not looking at me.

'But why didn't you say?'

'I wasn't here,' Joe told me with a shrug. 'Neither was Maria—she'd gone out to the market. It was that new boy we have who took the message.'

'For me?'

'He *asked* for you. According to the lad— what he said was—did a young lady called Miss Brown or something or other live here— one who sang and danced at nights?' and the boy said no, he hadn't heard o' one, there was only a guest, he said, a rich lookin' lady with a deep voice, not a singin' one at all. An' he doubted she could dance. She was kind o' proud, an' a bit buxom-like. He'd not heard her name, he said. Well, it was true, wasn't it?' Joe looked up and eyed me quizzically. 'You never *do* sing now, and you don't converse much either, and the lad'd only bin here two days.'

'I can't sing,' I said. 'My throat's still a bit raw. But I wish you'd told me before, Joe. How long ago was it?'

'A week or so,' he said. 'I didn't think it was that important. *Is* it?'

'It could be,' I replied evasively. 'It could be something to do with Signor Luigi, I suppose.'

'Oh. That Italiano. But he don't matter to you any more does he?'

'If—when—when I *do* recover properly,' I said, 'and I shall, I'm sure I shall—'

'Then you'll be here with *us*, won't you? Isn't that what was arranged? Once you was better you said, you'd be part of the Golden Bird like 'twas in the past.'

'Yes,' I said, feeling suddenly miserable. 'Of course.'

The matter was dropped there outwardly, but I knew the time was coming for a change. Either I had to tell Maria about the baby, or find a future somewhere else. But where? And what would I do? Somehow I had to make a living. 'Oh Rupert,' I thought, 'why didn't you stay here longer? Why didn't you wait to see Joe or Maria? And where are you? Why did you have to go away?'

The string of questions rang through my brain ceaselessly. But it was not until a week later that I found courage to face Maria with

191

the truth.

'I have to leave, Maria dear,' I told her one evening before the taproom opened. 'Oh, I'm sorry. I know I can never properly repay you for all you've done for me, but—I have to find Mr Verne.'

She started at me for seconds before making any comment. I could feel her gaze searching my face. Then she said, 'I see. So it's him.'

'Him? What do you mean?'

'You know very well. Part of you's been with us since you landed here those months' ago, but not your heart, girl. Oh, you're fond of us, but being fond's a different kind o' thing to loving. And I reckon you love that rich gentleman, for all he's left you wantin' and longin'.'

'No, he didn't leave me. I left him,' I stated flatly. 'Because he didn't need me enough, and because of his wife. She hated me, and things happened that weren't—good. Strange, dreadful things. I think she was at the back of them all.'

Maria sighed.

'Then for heaven's sake why d'you want to return? 'Specially when he probably isn't there. I've told you what the lad said, how he was always taking off up country. What's the sense of going back then? You tell me that.'

'There isn't always sense in loving, I suppose,' I admitted, feeling the old knot of pain at my heart. 'It just happens and once it's there, there's no way of stopping it. You go on, and on, and try to think the world's the same place, but it isn't—it never could be. These few months I've tried to harden myself against it, I have *tried*. But, Maria, what's the point when—when—' I stumbled over my words, hesitated, while she questioned, 'Go on, when what, girl?'

'When I'm going to have a baby,' I blurted out.

There was a long pause; my heart steadied gradually, relief at telling her made me suddenly more relaxed and content. When I looked at her face she was shaking her head, astonishment slowly giving place to acceptance of news that was distasteful to her.

'So that's it,' she said at last. 'The reason for it all—your silences and dizzy spells. I might've known.'

'No, how could you? You didn't expect it of me. Neither did I—I was always so—well, prim with the men, wasn't I, during the time I sang for you? But this is different, Maria,' I touched her hand tentatively. 'It's true, and real, and I couldn't fight against it—I *wouldn't* have anyway. From the first moment I saw him it started. How can I explain? I just can't. It was just—'

'A middle-aged man with gold in his pocket putting a spell on an innocent girl,' Maria interrupted tartly. 'Oh, I know the sort. But I wouldn't have expected it of him—not of Mr

193

Verne.'

'You don't know him. And it wasn't like that at all. Rather the other way round. I don't expect you to understand. But please *try*.'

Maria clasped her hands over her ample breasts. 'I don't know what Joe'll say. He'll be shocked, 'specially as he has a weak spot for you and expected you'd carry on here later as you did before.'

'Perhaps I will—later, when everything's over, the baby, I mean,' I told her. 'If you'll have me, that is. It all depends on Rupert. But you see now, don't you, why I have to go?'

'*No.* You could have the child here. This is a decent tavern. The child'd have a good home. There'd be no stintin' or scrapin'. —Whether you sang or not, you'd be good for the Golden Bird; you could help—'

'Not if Rupert wants me,' I said firmly.

'But, Josie, just get things straight in that muddle head o' yours. As you said yourself, he's married. His wife's sick and difficult— what d'you think your appearing in your state is going to do for him? Tell me that. Expect a welcome, do you? Then it's high time you had another think.'

But I was beyond thinking.

'I must go to Rupert,' I said. 'There are things I have to find out, and explain. I have to know what's been happening to him. I *have* to.'

'And *where* will you go? That there cottage of his? Or Kerrysmoor itself?' Her voice had become hard, bitter.

'No, I shall go to Truro first, The Crown where Rupert meant me to be when I left Tregonnis. They'll help me there, I'm sure they will, and I shall at least have news. There's Signor Luigi, too. He's sure to have knowledge of Rupert's affairs and whereabouts.'

At last, after further argument and protestations, Maria had to accept my decision. When Joe heard later, he was saddened rather than shocked; his attitude was more reasonable than Maria's, perhaps because men in certain circumstances have the aptitude for seeing things in a different light.

It was arranged, therefore, that I should take the postchaise from Falmouth for Truro the following week, on the understanding that if matters were unsatisfactory and didn't work out for me I would return immediately to the Golden Bird. Oh, they were good folk, and insisted on returning most of the payment I'd forced on them to help pay for my board at the inn.

'You take it,' Joe said, forcing a wallet into my hand when I was about to start off for the square where the chaise waited. 'You'll need it sure enough, in that fancy place. Put it in your valise now, an' don't let any pryin' Johnny know you've got it. Funny folk travels about nowadays.'

Gratitude almost brought tears to my eyes. I felt momentarily guilty at abandoning the two

195

people who'd grown to care for me almost as a daughter during the time I was with them.

Was I doing the wise thing? I didn't know, or really care. Ten minutes's later, to the clatter of wheels and hollow sound of horses' hooves, only one thought registered in my mind. I had started on the journey that in one way or another must bring me news of Rupert Verne.

CHAPTER ELEVEN

Although quite a time had passed since Rupert had written the note ensuring his responsibility for me at the inn, the landlord received me politely, and I was given a pleasant but old-fashioned bedroom, looking over a kind of courtyard bordered by a granite wall and a few almost leafless trees. There was a framed oleograph of General Gordon hanging on one wall, and a picture depicting Queen Victoria's coronation on another. Two angels escorting a little child in a nightgown to Heaven hung immediately over the heavy oak four-poster bed. The furniture was dark mahogany, and a smell of camphor mingled with the faint tang of malt permeated the air. The china ewer and basin on the washstand were patterned with pink roses, and the curtains were heavy crimson plush, on each side of a blind that rattled when pulled by a cord.

196

A framed religious text stood on the chest of drawers; I had no doubt that it was considered a privilege to occupy such a room, but a weary sense of depression fell on me. I felt smothered at first, with an almost hysterical urge to escape and somehow find transport to Tregonnis immediately.

But I managed to curb my impatience and to eat the ample evening meal provided of roast beef, vegetables, and apple pie.

I didn't think I'd manage to sleep well in the stuffy surroundings, but I did, I was too exhausted to keep awake, and in the morning after a good breakfast of gruel and boiled ham, I made enquiries about Signor Luigi.

'Luigi?' the manageress asked me, arching her heavy black brows over a hawk-like nose. 'You meant the proud little Italiano?—the music teacher?'

'Yes. I have to contact him.'

She was a stout woman with her dark hair piled high over a plump pink face. Gold rings dangled from her ears, jet beads and locket decorated her large bosom.

'He is a friend of Mr Verne's,' I explained, 'and was giving me singing lessons until—well, until my throat became bad—I had a fever you see, and had to stop them. But it's important I contact him now. Which is the quickest way to his home? I feel like walking, and—'

'Oh, but you won't find him there now,' the plump woman stated very definitely, 'He's

197

gone.'

'*Gone?*'

She shrugged. There was something Spanish about her, nonchalant and slightly contemptuous, as though a famous maestro was of no consequence to the clientele of the hostelry.

'That's what I said,' she told me. 'You never know when those foreigners are likely to take off. He'll be back, of course, sometime; he often does it in the winter—prefers a bit of sun on the continent to the cold here. I don't blame him, being a free man, *if* he is. But then you never know, do you? He could have a wife or a woman tucked away in Italy.' She paused, eyeing me shrewdly, 'Was your business important with him, Miss—Miss—?'

'Lebrun,' I answered. 'Josephine Lebrun.'

'Ah yes. I remember now.' She folded her arms and regarded me knowingly.

'And my business wasn't important,' I added, before she could get another question in. 'Not with Signor Luigi. The person I really have to contact is my—my—' I searched for the right word and miraculously found it '—my sponsor, whose name you have, Mr Verne. First of all, though, before going to Kerrysmoor, I have to call at Tregonnis.'

Her jaw dropped. 'Isn't that the place, the cottage where—where that dreadful thing happened?'

'What dreadful thing?' I asked sharply.

198

'What do you mean? What's happened?'

Her mouth tightened into a small button.

'Ah. That's what we'd all like to know. But if you go there you'll certainly have a shock, Miss—Miss Lebrun. As for Mr Verne—it's hardly likely you'll find him at Kerrysmoor. Not at the moment.'

'But *why*? You *must* explain.'

'Pardon me!' she said in ridiculously haughty tones. 'There's no must about it. I gave my solemn word to Master Verne to keep my mouth shut about things going on in that bad place—we all have. All of us here. Of course, there are all manners of rumours spreading, some may be true, some not. But if you take my advice you'll stay here for a time until Mr Verne makes it his business to contact you. When you didn't turn up before he was very put out, and called here twice. It was, if I may say so, a little thoughtless of you to go wandering about when you were under his protection. Still, that's not my affair. I have collateral, and assurances from him that any expenses incurred by you will be amply repaid. You are, in a way, under our protection. I hope you get my meaning, Miss Lebrun.'

Yes, I got her meaning, and I had not the slightest intention of complying with it.

At the first opportunity I decided to sneak out of the Crown and somehow make my way to Tregonnis.

The opportunity arrived that same

afternoon. A November mist hung heavily over the streets of Truro, and with my valise packed, and wearing my brown cape over the warmest and most inconspicuous gown I had with me, I made my way softly down the stairs, tip-toed past the parlour where the landlady was having her beverage of tea, laced, I guessed, with something stronger.

A wave of foggy air greeted me as I stepped into the street. Any traffic there was, crawled. Figures were mere blurred shapes passing by. This was all to my advantage. No one would be likely to notice the indeterminate figure of a woman passing with chin sunk into dark clothing, just one chilly pedestrain among others making her way to some vague destination. I walked aimlessly for a time, simply taking any corner that appeared unexpectedly willy-nilly, uncaring of where it led. At one point I tried to hail a cab, but the jarvy was huddled into his coat and passed unheedingly, which perhaps was as well. I was getting short of funds, and realised that I'd probably need all I'd got for cheaper transport covering a longer distance. Tregonnis was a considerable distance from Truro—a fact that I'd not properly considered before.

At last I came to the outskirts of the city. The lights that had feebly illuminated the streets before, had flickered out one by one. All now was hushed and grey, and dark. Hedges, the occasional distorted shape of a building or shed came into looming blurred visibility then faded again, taken into coils of thick vapour. A damp river smell crept from low land to the road, and I had a brief glimpse of what could have been water lying beyond a clump of bushes. The next moment it had gone. I walked on mechanically for some way, chilled and a little frightened, knowing I had behaved unreasonably. It would have been wiser to have waited until the morning when the fog might have cleared. How would I reach Tregonnis in such weather? How would I find shelter of any kind to help me on my way?

I was debating whether to turn and somehow find my way back to the Crown when a beam of reddish light straggled through the mist some distance ahead of me. As I drew closer I realised it filtered from somewhere round a bend in the roadway, carrying with it a distant malty smell characteristic of a tavern or kiddleywink. Relief filled me. An inn of any kind must provide temporary warmth and shelter.

I quickened my steps, and was taking the corner when a broad shape lumbered against me, swaying and muttering obscenities. I almost fell, but managed to step aside and plunge on, with the reeking smell of spirits thick in my nostrils. The inn stood on my left. There was a sign of some sort swinging over the door, making a creaking sound that became peculiarly interrupted with the rise and fall of voices and raucous laughter from inside. Remembering to keep my reticule safely close in an inner pocket of my cape, I entered. The air inside was thick and cloying, steamy with male breath and beer. I hesitated before entering the tap room, and put my valise down for a moment to easy my aching arm. It was then that a burly figure emerged from the bar, obviously on the point of leaving. In the glow of the reddish oil lamp his face showed a rubicund and rustic kindliness that somehow suggested he could be a local man, probably a farmer, and that he was not inebriated.

'Well!' he exclaimed in a Cornish burr, 'a lady, on a night like this, an' alone. Where ee bin from, m'dear, and where ee be too? Tedn' a right place for ee in theer. Travellin'? Eh?'

In a rush, because I had no one else to confide in, and he appeared honest enough, I told him I had to get to Tregonnis that night somehow, that I could pay a certain amount for transport, and that if he knew of anyone willing to take me, or a waggon—

'It's very important,' I urged. 'I was wondering whether to stay here, if they could put me up, and then start off early when the light was better. But what I have in my—in my bag—isn't enough for a proper bedroom and food, and—and—' I broke off desperately, knowing I was making a poor exhibition of myself.

A large palm descended on my shoulder.

'Midear young wumman, this place edn' for the like of you, an' like as not theers no space 'tall for virtue this night. A man o' any kind c'n take care of isself, but *you*?' He gave a gruff laugh, 'Now tell you what, chile, I can't say I've heard tell o' this 'ere Tregonnis you do speak of, but I've me cart outside an' good stout mare. Goin' westwards I am, ef I can give ee a ride—alongside, I'll do et willin', an' no questions asked. No pay neither. Joseph Killiwarne I be, an' the Killiwarne's is honest farmin' folk—'

Well, I accepted the offer gratefully, and minutes later I was once more setting off, with someone I'd never seen or heard of before, into the dark and thickening Cornish night. He'd said westwards, and Tregonnis was to the west, in the direction of the wild North Coast.

We'd been driving only a few minutes before he asked, 'Where's it near to? This Tre—Tre-whatsit?—you mentioned?'

'Kerrysmoor,' I told him. 'Mr—Mr Verne's place.'

'*Ah! Him.*'

'Do you know him by any chance?'

'Only by repute midear, as they say. 'Bin trouble like, I do b'lieve. Some wumman.'

My heart sank. I felt suddenly so very alone and lost again.

'Oh. I had heard but wasn't sure what the trouble was. But I—' I thought up as reasonable an explanation as I could. 'I used to work there. And I've business to discuss.'

'I see. I see. Tedn' my affair midear. Whatever business you do have mus' be important to get you goin' theer on a night like this. Funny weather. I doan altogether like et. Could be a storm comin', one o' they freak kind you doan quite know what t'expect. Bein' used to the land an' its ways, I got a nose for this sort o' thing. Ais!—a storm brewin' for sure.' He paused, and when I said nothing, continued, 'Know Tharne, do ee?'

'Oh *yes*,' I exclaimed. 'Tharne isn't far from Tregonnis. If you could put me down there, I'd be perfectly all right.'

'Depend on th' fog,' the man said. 'We'll see. I've a nephew theer, callin' on him I am, before tekkin' off 'gain, f'r Penzance way.'

I didn't ask his nephew's name, or probe in any way about his business. Neither did I comment on the fact that it was unusual for any farmer to be making such a journey at so late an hour. It wasn't my affair. He could be involved in any lucrative sideline. What lay under cover at the back of his cart was his concern and his alone, whether of a legal or smuggling nature.

So we clattered on down unknown ways and turns stopping only occasionally to give the horse a rest, while Joe Killiwarne took a nip of whisky from a bottle, and forced a little on me.

Very gradually the fog lifted considerably, revealing, as the man had predicted, a sullen belt of black cloud, blanketing the night sky. Everything was very still, but occasionally the clouds parted to reveal a thin stream of watery moonlight emphasising the deep gloom of approaching rain.

When we reached Tharne he offered to take me on to Tregonnis after his business with his nephew was over. But I refused.

'It's only a short distance,' I told him, 'and once I reach the main road I can soon be there. I don't want to waste any time or hurry you. I'm very grateful for the lift.'

I offered him payment once more, but he wouldn't accept it, and following a few more polite and cursory remarks we parted, and I was on my way towards the cottage.

The light became eerie. The overhanging heavy sky seemed to lower as an insidious rustling wind scurried along the ground swirling what remaining mist there was in grey coils over the wet earth. A few dead leaves tapped my ankles; the surface of the nearby stream quivered into glassy brilliance for brief seconds when shafts of silver-green moonlight momentarily pierced the massed clouds before dying again into stygian blackness. I found my way more from habit than sight. Every moment I half expected to hear the clip-clop of hooves and heavy wheels of Joe Killiwarne's cart approaching. If I had, then I'd have taken an offer of a lift for the rest of the way to Tregonnis if it was still forthcoming. But there was no sound of human presence or activity—only a low rumble of thunder from the distance and intermittent flashes of lightning.

Soon spatters of rain intensified. The wind rose, and I pulled the hood of my cape well down over my head, pushing my hair beneath. As the storm properly broke, realisation of my own folly swept over me. Who would have thought though, that from such an over-quiet misty afternoon and evening, such a deluge could arise? And why hadn't I waited until the morning before making my reckless journey to Tregonnis? Who or what did I expect to find there?

There was only one answer. Rupert. Rupert—Rupert—I almost called his name aloud. Surely something of him—some sign of his presence, or that he had been there—must await me at the cottage?

I pushed on, while the rain increased into torrential force. When I took the turn in the main lane leading round the base of Rosecarrion I was already soaked to the skin. The wind had become a savage elemental force whipping its fury against me, and as a tree crashed down ahead, my head rang with the mocking illusion of wild fiendish laughter—the triumphant screeching of the Three Maidens. Gasping for breath and trying to wipe the dripping water from my eyes, I clutched at the twisted trunk of a bush for support. The ground seemed to rock beneath my feet, and when I tried to move on I was helpless against the holocaust. How long it was before the storm gradually eased enabling me to continue, I had no idea. Thunder still rolled ominously through the air and my boots were ankle-deep in mud when at last I reached the gates of Tregonnis. Moonlight zig-zagged across the path, or where the path had once been.

I blinked, screwed my eyes up, and looked again, hardly believing what I saw. An acrid bitter smell rose from the boggy earth. Rocks and stones were strewn about everywhere, and the building was just a hump of debris—no more. The outhouse—where I'd thought I could shelter if there was no one there and the door was locked against me—was merely a blackened pile of fallen granite and timber. The cottage too,—there was nothing; just nothing but charred relics of what once had been a dwelling.

I rubbed my eyes, wondering if I was suffering from some strange hallucination, but the ravaged scene only appeared intensified. A feeling of weakness made me lean against a blackened stump of tree, and slowly the fit of trembling ceased. I knew I had to get away as soon as possible. Nothing remained there but desolation; I had either to find my way back to Tharne where some cottage might provide refuge until the morning—or take the turn along the main road to Kerrysmoor.

Presumably someone was in residence there—if not Rupert or Lady Verne—servants who'd take me in. To wait longer in my wet and shivering state could be dangerous not only for myself, but for the child I was carrying.

So I forced myself from the gate, and with my head bowed into my cape, made my way down the lane to the road. The rain slowly ceased at last, leaving the black and savage landscape washed to luminous sinister clarity from the moon which was now fully risen. Cold! everything appeared cold and clearly cut—black and lemon silver-white, as though a cruel giant hand had swept Nature free of growth and future life. A dead land. No bird even cried or flapped its wings from the beaten undergrowth. There was no sound but a dripping and murmuring of water trickling in streams and rivulets from the moor.

At last in its darkened valley I saw the turreted shape of Kerrysmoor crouched beneath the hill. I stood for a few seconds to get my breath and gather more strength before taking the turn leading upwards to the house. As I walked up the avenue and joined the drive, I lifted my head and stared upwards, at the stretch of wild moorland rising from the back of the mansion, to its rugged summit where the vividly silhouetted shapes of the Three Maidens stood.

There they were—primeval, stark against the cold sky, emitting a malignant elemental force that to my heightened nerves heralded disaster. Long shadows streaked like clawing gigantic fingers down the slope. At the same time I heard an ominous rumble as though the earth itself was shuddering in response. Then, before I could force myself ahead, I saw it—a dot of black, with arms outspread to the moonlight. It wavered and jigged against the sky, before leaping and jumping downwards towards the house.

Terror held me rooted where I was. I thought at first I must be in a nightmare or had lost my senses, as my fixed gaze detected another—either human being or some distorted creature of the night scrambling and crawling up the moor for combat or greeting. And as I watched, the trembling of the earth intensified. Horrified, I saw the great stones— the Three Maidens—move convulsively from their beds and with the crashing and roaring of Nature come rolling, tumbling down the moor, accompanied by great boulders and an eruption of earth and stones that claimed the dots of figures, bringing them in their landslide of destruction to the valley.

Rivers ran; the far wall of Kerrysmoor collapsed. Above the thundering and screaming of rocks and debris, I seemed to hear a frail human crying for help.

Why I thought of Rupert I don't know. But suddenly, with terrifying certainty—a knowledge far beyond human sense or reasoning, I knew he was there—dying maybe, and needing me. I ran then, rushed with an energy I'd not known I possessed—stumbling, crawling, getting to my feet again, and going ahead, climbing over mounds of mud, forcing myself against the angry streams of stones, shale and wrenched undergrowth, to the great wall of erupted moor where any victims of the avalanche must be. Sometimes I had to sink breathless to the boggy ground, clearing my eyes of dust and mud. Once I glanced back and saw the creeping filth claiming the near wall and roof of Kerrysmoor—an immense tide of hungry destruction.

I went on again, pulling myself up by any projecting root of tree or rock available, and at last, beyond the barrier came to a pit already half-filled with still slipping boulders. I slid some yards down, and then saw them—the Three Maidens. One was half upright, the other two sucked to the ground, almost submerged by rubble. The largest lay over the dot of a victim—a human figure with gaping mouth in its distorted face, entangled in reddened debris. I could have vomited, but forced myself to look away.

And then I had the worst shock of all. Only a few yards ahead was the body of a man lying flat on his back, with a stream of blood coursing from his head. A rock lay over one leg which was twisted at a distorted angle from the knee. Despite the fitful wan scene which at times flared still from flashes of receding lightning blending with the moon's glow, the features were clear and could have been those of some legendary knight resurrected from his tomb. The rest of his form was caked with thick mud.

Rupert.

I knelt down, whispering and crying his name, pressing my face to his own cold wounded countenance. He didn't stir; only a flicker of an eye-lid gave an indication at all that he still lived.

Despair filled me. I had to get help somehow. But from where? The part of Kerrysmoor facing the moor was gone, submerged by the elemental upheaval. Tregonnis was empty and a ruin. The farm? But God alone knew what had happened to that, and it was some distance off. I searched the landscape wildly, then turned my eyes again to the victims, recalling that there were two. The other—a woman— was obviously dead, completely crushed by the great stones on top of her. Her eyes were blank, wild and staring; a claw-like hand, greenish-white, was clutched round the handle of a knife, reddened by blood. Lady Verne.

I put my hands to my eyes, struggling to keep control of my nerves, and then, after getting to my feet, started running, slipping, sliding, crawling, jumping, sometimes slithering in streams of earth, until I came to a mound of bricks, mortar and granite that had once been

211

the whole back portion of Kerrysmoor.

Somehow I found my way to a winding lane of slush that had been the road. Driven by an urgency stronger than exhaustion, fear or limitation of my own strength I pressed on, and eventually saw a small crowd of rescuers plodding to the scene of the disaster.

'He's there—' I managed to gasp before I collapsed, 'injured under a rock—the Three Maidens—and her, Lady Verne. Save him— save Rupert—'

I could continue no more. Suddenly the whole world seemed to fade into darkness; there was a roaring in my ears, and I fell, mercifully into unconsciousness.

* * *

When I came to myself I was lying on a sofa in the housekeeper's parlour at Kerrysmoor. A small group of locals were standing in the hall, near the door which opened to a path leading to a side drive. I could feel the sting of something warm in my throat, and saw Mrs Treen carrying a flask and glass to the table.

It took me some moments to recall what had happened, and when I remembered, I sat up and cried shrilly, 'Rupert?—Mr Verne—have you—have they found him?'

Mrs Treen took me by the shoulders and forced me to lie back. 'The Master's badly hurt,' she told me, 'but still alive, thank the good Lord.'

'*Hurt*? Of course. I know that. Where *is* he?'

'In the study. Washed and clean as possible,' she answered. 'The doctor will be here soon as somethin' can get going along the lane—no more than a mud track it is now, and as for the house—' she threw up her hands—'just half of it left, if that.'

'And her ladyship?' Even in such terrible circumstances I could not keep the bitterness out of my voice.

'She's—she's beyond what this world can do to her any more,' the woman answered. 'They've put her in the back parlour, poor thing. You saw her though, didn't you?'

I nodded, feeling a sudden shame at my own hardness. But the knife clenched in the thin hand, and the expression of the face—how could I feel pity for Lady Verne when it had obviously been her intention to harm Rupert?

All other thoughts were swept away as I remembered how still he'd lain in the moonlight—how ravaged as though dead.

'I'd like to see Mr Verne,' I said, 'please let me.'

The housekeeper shook her head. 'No one'll see Master Verne until the doctor's been. *No* one. He's in a coma of sorts, and anyway what right have you?'

'It's not a matter of *right*. It's—I *found* him. I was *there*.'

'Well, I hope you're not going to be difficult,'

Mrs Treen said severely. 'I'm housekeeper here, and in charge. When the doctor comes we'll see. But everyone's had a shock remember—I'm not feeling too good myself. No one is. Fanny, that new housemaid swooned and had hysterics—and William, the footman, slipped in the rubble and broke his leg. So it's up to you, including all the rest, to act as normal as possible without argument. It's a mercy any of this place is left, but we've the kitchens, the dining room and the front parlour, and the main staircase is left—at the bottom; some bedrooms too. How many no one knows yet, nor how any roof or walls stayed. Cornish granite though—that's what my da always said, you can't beat Cornish granite for putting up a fight against storm—'

She babbled on as though she'd never stop talking; I guessed it was shock; no one else could get a word in until the doctor arrived, and then, when she'd taken him to where Rupert lay, she returned, and suddenly collapsed by the fire place, her skin turned a ghastly green colour, with her eyes closed. One of the rescuers, a man I knew by sight, who'd worked in the grounds, rushed to her aid, and heaved her into a chair. I grabbed the flask from the table, and he forced a drink on her; she revived, made a feeble effort to push him away, and muttered, 'Don't fuss me up. I'm all right. And look at you—all mud and dirty marks on the floor—'

He smiled grimly, and replaced the brandy. Tiredness claimed me again. I slumped back on the sofa, and gradually warmth from the fire soothed me once more into a half state of consciousness. I was aware of movement, of comings and goings, the murmur of voices, but until the arrival of the doctor nothing seemed to matter. All I wanted was to rest and drift into forgetfulness.

The rest of the night passed like a jumbled half-dream. When morning came Mrs Treen had recovered sufficiently to give orders to the bewildered and shocked staff. Breakfast was served in the kitchen, and attempts made to clean up what remained at Kerrysmoor. Rupert, I learned, had had his leg straightened and dressed, and his wound attended to. The doctor had said that later he'd have to see a specialist from Truro about the leg, but so far as he himself could judge, no irretrievable damage had been done.

How wrong they were.

When at last I was allowed to see him, it appeared at first he was his old self. A bed had been made comfortable for him in the study, and he was lying half-propped up with the injured limb bandaged and stiff before him, a bandage over his temple. He smiled, as after a light knock, I entered. There was a glow in his yellow-gold eyes that told me all was well between us.

'Oh Rupert—' I cried, running towards him,

'you're better—you'll be all right. I thought at first you were—you'd died.'

'*Died?*' He gave a short laugh which held also a wince of pain. 'It takes more than a thunderstorm to kill a hardened adventurer like me. Don't look so shocked, Melissa—'

I was puzzled. '*Melissa?*'

'That's your name, isn't it? You can't be called darling all the time.'

'I—I don't—'

'Come on, my love. No games. It seems to me—' and he stared at me reflectively, with just a hint of teasing in his glance, 'since you sat for that portrait you've got slightly—shall we say, above yourself?' His voice was mocking, but warm and caring.

'Rupert—' I began, puzzled. 'I'm *not* Melissa—I'm—oh don't you remember? Josephine, Josephine Lebrun—?'

I broke off, trembling, waiting and fearing his answer.

He said nothing for a moment, then replied, 'Another little act? *Don't*, love, *please.* Not just now. I've had a fall, remember? My horse slipped, and this damned leg's giving me hell. Yes, sweetheart, you're a very good actress, and one day—' He didn't finish, exhaustion overcame him, the lids fluttered down over his eyes, and I realised he was asleep.

Mrs Treen came to the door. 'You've been long enough,' she said acidly. 'You know what I told you, what the doctor said, you could

216

have just a glance and pass a word or two if he spoke, but it seems to me you've had a good old chatter.'

I shook my head. 'No—he thought I was someone else, that's all.'

My voice must have betrayed the desolation I felt; her expression softened and changed.

'Oh?'

That one word was a question.

'Yes. Someone called Melissa.'

Was it my fancy, or did what little colour she had, suddenly fade from her face?

'Well,' she said after a pause, 'the Master's known many folk—gentlemen *and* ladies in his time. He's had a great shock remember, and that gash on his temple may've set him rambling a bit. Anyway, it's not *your* worry, girl, and seems to me I've done wrong to let you bother him at all. Now come along. You look whisht enough yourself. And I don't want invalids around me, there's enough to do getting what we can in order here. There'll be the funeral to arrange too.'

'*Funeral?*' I gasped.

The housekeeper's mouth went prim, almost condemning.

'Have you forgotten her ladyship? The Master won't be able to attend, if I'm any judge, but all who are fit should see they pay due respects.' She eyed me severely. 'Including *you*. Between them the Master and Lady Verne have done a good deal on your behalf, girl.'

217

'*He* had,' I admitted sharply. 'But she always hated me.'

The next moment I knew I shouldn't have spoken so, and before she could reply I'd swept from the room and made my way to the hall and out of the door to what remained of the grounds that side, and the lane.

Destruction was everywhere. Though the mud had drifted and dried in patches on the road, trees and bushes were broken from the onslaught, rocks were strewn about, streams still trickled in rivulets of filth from the devastated area of moorland behind the house. The freshened clarity of cold paper-clear skies, only emphasised the desolation—a desolation magnified by despair and the loss of an illusion in my own heart.

It was Melissa Rupert loved.

Not me.

CHAPTER TWELVE

During the weeks that followed I stayed on at Kerrysmoor to help Mrs Treen in the extra work involved by the landslide. At first I'd thought I'd be sent away, and had made tentative plans to return to the Golden Bird, but when the housekeeper made it clear I could be of use to her, I agreed willingly—not only on her account but because of Rupert. There was

218

Dame Jenny, too, who had mercifully been spared, but had become a semi-invalid.

The considerable part of the house that remained was comparatively untouched, but the constant walking to and fro of workmen employed in building a back wall as ballast for the surviving wings of the mansion, and for levelling as effectively as possible the hundredweights of rubble left, meant continual extra cleaning and brushing up. There was as well the carrying up of trays to the bedroom where Rupert was taken following the first two days spent in the library, and to Dame Jenny. A specialist, who came from Truro, sent a nurse along for a week or two. She also had to be looked after, and Mrs Treen daily seemed to be showing more strain. The housemaid had left, and only a small staff remained, so I would not, in any case, have deserted her.

My brief meetings with Rupert were poignant and painful—not only physically to him, but because he struggled so hard to get well, and because he continued to think of me as Melissa. I corrected him once, but when he clearly thought I was joking, I knew he didn't recall there had ever been a girl in his life called Josephine Lebrun. Only that other—the girl in the portrait.

At Mrs Treen's request I had attended Lady Verne's funeral held at St Clemo's Church in a nearby village. It was a grey day. My spine felt rigid and cold from strain and the chill wind blowing. Except for myself only two or three servants and a few natives attended. I was thankful when the sordid ceremony was over, and I was once more in the carriage driving back to Kerrysmoor.

One day when Jan called with eggs, I asked him about Tregonnis. 'What happened *there*? Was *that* a landslide, too?'

We were standing outside the house on the path. He looked round cautiously in every direction as if he wished no-one to hear his answer, then replied, 'Haven't they told you then?'

I shook my head. 'There's been so much else going on, and whenever I brought the question up, Mrs Treen pretended not to hear and changed the subject. It was the same with the other servants—the two men.'

Jan shrugged. 'I do suppose they'd bin given orders earlier,' he said, 'when she was sick like.'

'Sick? Who?'

'*Her*. The dead woman—Master's wife, Lady Verne. She'd gone funny in the head, an' so I've heard was took up country to some place where they have mad folk. Then she got away—'

'Escaped, you mean?'

He nodded.

'That's right. An' it was her—*her* who set fire to Tregonnis. I heard from him, ole Johnny Trink—only nobody says, nat'ruly. An' if you ask me—' his voice lowered, 'she'd gone real *murderous*. Seems unfair, doan' et? A man like Master, travelling up country just to see her all right—an' then her havin' a go at him like that.'

'I see,' I said slowly. 'So *that* was it.'

'What, miss?'

'The reason for him being away so much.'

'O' course. Only we wasn' supposed to know, or speak of it. Some do say though she was a witch. An' tell you the truth, missie, one night at full moon I did see her dancin' like in a queer way round they ole stones, the Three Maidens, just as though she was one o' them. All in black she was, wearin' a dark hood thing—an' I recognised her. Oh yes, I knowed it was her. Quite near I was, lookin' for a lost lamb. I told em 'bout it at th' farm. But they said as how I shouldn' go spreadin' tales, but keep me mouth shut—'cos after all she was Master Verne's lady wife, and harm'd hit us if I said anythin' bad 'bout her.'

'I don't believe she had any power to hurt you, Jan,' I said in a sudden spurt of commonsense, 'and I don't believe the Three Maidens were anything but old stones, either.'

'No?'

'That's what I said.'

'But they was once young women what was enchanted 'cos they danced on a Sabbath. That's what I heard from my ole granny. Turned into stone they wuz, but stones havin'

221

strange powers o' wickedness at the full moon.'

'Just a story, a legend,' I told him. 'They *have* a *kind* of magic, I suppose—I've felt it myself, but it's just the age of them and the way they stood there on top of the moor. Imagination itself is a very strange thing, Jan, you must remember that.'

'An' was it imagination then what saved the picture?' Jan enquired in a knowing kind of way.

My heart jerked.

'What picture? What do you mean?' Even as I asked the question, I guessed.

'The one the Master had hung at Tregonnis—the lady with the bright hair. He fair worshipped her, he did. An' et's funny edn' et? Although everythin' else was burned in the fire, her face wasn'. Just that one bit saved. Just her face.'

I went cold all over.

'Where is it now?'

'I dunno. I reckon Mrs Treen's got it somewhere. I heard the Master give it to her for safe keepin', away from his wife. Just because of her madness you know, she had a real hate of it. So it was a *kind* of magic saved *that*, wasn't it?—a magic stronger than the witches' put together. An' I reckon that's religion, doan' you, miss? The *real* kind, meanin' the power of good over evil?'

'Perhaps you're right,' I admitted. 'Yes. And try to remember it.'

He nodded and started to walk away.

'Jan—' I called.

He turned his head, 'Yes, miss?'

'Who was she? The lady in the portrait? And what was her name?'

'I never knowed her,' he said.

'But you called her beautiful. So—'

'My mam said so. Everyone knowed it, but no one talks of her 'cos the Master forbid it.'

I sighed, and he went on his way, leaving me feeling bereft, lonely and bewildered, by a mystery that seemed to me then beyond solving.

Once or twice later during the week I sounded Mrs Treen as tactfully as possible about the matter, but she refused point blank to give any information or even answer me except to say, 'I've told you before to mind your own business about things that don't concern you.'

Little she knew how very much I *was* concerned, although I was beginning to realise that quite soon I should have to confide in her about the child I carried. For some time I'd taken pains to conceal as effectively as possible the thickening of my figure by wearing a full apron-front to a full blue dress I'd been careful to bring along with me from the Golden Bird. Somehow it had survived all my adventures. Joe Burns' remark to me before leaving Falmouth, about his new employee's description of me as a plumpish, haughty-like

223

young woman, following Rupert's enquiry, had made me aware that I must be increasingly vigilant over my shape. But the truth couldn't be hidden for ever, and I wondered what would happen when I told Mrs Treen. She mightn't want me there anymore—probably wouldn't. And if I mentioned Rupert—but how could I when he was still ill and thought of me as Melissa?

When I wasn't working, the problem went round and round in my head, and I began to sleep badly.

'What's the matter with you these days?' the housekeeper asked one morning, when I couldn't eat my breakfast. A sudden nausea seized me. I got up and rushed from the room. She followed, and panting reached me as I stumbled into my bedroom. I stood over the basin at the washstand, vomited, but nothing came of the effort. I just felt faint and ill, and slumped on to the bed.

'Now you'd better be straight about this,' I heard her saying firmly, in a manner that was almost an accusation. 'You're expectin', aren't you?'

I nodded bleakly, and for a moment didn't speak. Then life returned to me, and courage from the relief of confession. 'Yes,' I said, lifting my head and facing her with a certain defiance. 'And please don't tell me I should be ashamed, because I'm not.'

'That's why you left Falmouth, I suppose,'

she said primly, 'to come here and dump your—your—' She struggled to get the odious word 'bastard' out, or possibly 'by-blow', but before she could do so I'd stopped her by interrupting:

'You needn't say it. I know very well what you think. It's no matter now. The baby will be loved and brought up properly, I'll see to that—somehow I'll see to it. I will, I *will*—'

'And how? Where? In the back streets of Falmouth?' she snorted contemptuously. 'You've been a fool, girl.'

'Maybe,' I agreed. 'In your opinion. Not mine. You see I *loved* the father. And when you love—'

'Then where is he? This seducer of young women who cares so much for his own appetite he leaves one like you to bring his bastard into the world without means or a name to face the world. *Love*! I'm surprised at *you*—you'd respect from a fine family, and a grand singing career mapped out for you, looks and—yes, I'll admit it—a certain presence—and yet you throw it all away because some lying, lusting male takes you like any—any—'

'*Stop*!' I cried. 'I won't listen. I'll—'

'You'll tell me his name, girl. An' if it's anyone known round here I'll see he pays for it.'

I almost laughed in her face. Anyone that was *known*! The whole picture was ludicrous. If I said, 'Well, for your satisfaction, it's the

225

Master, Mr Rupert Verne', how would she have reacted? *Believed* me? Or accused me of lying and sent me packing there and then? Who could say? She might even have had a stroke and died. And anyway what good could have come of bringing Rupert's name into it when he already remembered nothing of me at all?

From that point I refused point-blank to discuss the matter further, except for immediate domestic plans. In the end the irate housekeeper soothed down, following a glass of a special concoction she kept to calm nerves and ward off an attack of the megrims. The result was that because she needed me just then, I could stay on, provided I managed to keep my condition quiet until necessity demanded otherwise. Then we'd have to have another 'think' she said.

There really wouldn't be any thinking to do, I decided later, when I was on my own. I'd return to the Golden Bird. Joe and Maria would take me in, and the baby could be born in comparative comfort. In the meantime, perhaps there'd be a miracle, and Rupert would remember.

Christmas came and went. I saw very little of Rupert, simply because he kept mostly to his own quarters upstairs, and partly due to my own embarrassment. He could not yet go riding, or even walking more than a quarter of a mile, and it was painful to me to have to witness so pronounced a limp in a man who before had been so active, hardy and athletic.

Whenever we met, by chance in the house or garden, he would regard me with a warm but puzzled look in his eyes. Once he asked, 'Why do you avoid me, Melissa? You know I still care for you. Another thing—is it wise to leave Tregonnis so often? It could be dangerous for you under the circumstances. I had to do it you know—' His voice trailed off as he wrinkled his brow trying to remember something I knew could be a vital link in the mystery that separated us.

'Had to do what, Rupert?' I asked.

'Marry Alicia,' he answered dully.

'Oh yes, of course,' I said.

'If it hadn't been for that damned war I'd never have left, and you'd have been all right. You wouldn't have—' he put his hand to his head. 'Oh God, what am I saying? Leave me, Melissa, I'm all at sea. But I shall remember in time; heaven help me, I will.'

I tried to think he was right, although his confusion not only worried, but frightened me badly.

The doctor, who called every week, said only time would show how deep the injury to his brain was. There might be nothing permanent at all. His physical condition was remarkable considering what he'd been through—although again, the fractured leg might never completely recover.

When I asked Mrs Treen about Rupert's

references to the war, she replied, 'Oh yes, the Master had served in the Crimea and been a very brave soldier. He'd been away a year, and during that time his elder brother, Lucas, had died, after playing ducks and drakes with the estate.'

Although such information didn't explain Melissa, it did give a possible clue for his reason in marrying Lady Alicia—provided of course she had means for assisting him in getting the estate into order again. I didn't like seeing him in any mercenary light, but then Rupert was the kind of man who once he had set his mind on a thing there was little he wouldn't do to achieve it. If only he could have wanted me that much. Oh, if only something would happen to bring us together. Even now, though insisting he cared for me, he didn't see me as I was—but as Melissa, the girl in the portrait. And I didn't look like her—not a bit. No wonder he was confused and moody, looking at me lovingly one moment, the next suspiciously, as though resentful of my presence.

One day, when I was dusting and tidying the library, he limped in unexpectedly, and said, 'I like you in that dress, it suits you—the colour of your eyes.'

I went towards him and he pulled me to him for a second, kissed me, then inexplicably pushed me away.

'What's the matter?' I asked, 'Why did

you—why don't you—don't you like me any more?'

His golden eyes narrowed and darkened, became slits of condemnation. '*Like*? What a word to use. Don't dare make such a tom-fool remark again.'

'Rupert—I—'

'And don't argue, for God's sake. You know we can never marry. But there's no point in rubbing it in. And another thing—'

'Yes?'

'Apart from the rest—the barrier—I'm a cripple.'

'I don't care what you are,' I told him recklessly. 'You say you love me, well I love you. And where's the barrier now? She's dead. Alicia's dead.'

'I don't know what you are talking about.'

The tone of his voice, set of his jaw and obvious dislike of talking with me at all, brought a lump to my throat.

'All right, Rupert—Mr Verne,' I said. 'I can see I'm annoying you. So I'll—I'll go—'

And I did.

I left him standing in angry posture, with his hands behind his back, morosely facing the fire. Depression weighed heavily on me. Just then I could see little hope for a happy outcome.

January followed into early February, sprinkling the earth with snowdrops. Christmas roses bloomed behind the house, and even signs of green pushed bravely through the ground where such destruction had been only a month or two ago. Most of the land had been levelled, though the gardens had been obliterated and would have to be replanned and made later, if Rupert wished. Workmen were still about, rebuilding the large wing under the moor, although on a smaller scale.

The man I'd loved so passionately and who before had appeared so dedicated to his estate now showed only a desultory interest, giving orders and directions when asked for, but in a bored way as though Kerrysmoor no longer vitally concerned him. I sympathised deeply with his concern and the shock he'd suffered, but his attitude of giving way so obviously to frustration, frequently irritated and almost goaded me into crying:

'Why don't you at least *try*?—why don't you *fight* and live again? You're alive and strong, and in time your leg will be normal—if it isn't, you'll still be able to get about and ride, and love me—*love*, Rupert! have you forgotten what it's like to hold me in your arms and kiss me, to take me in passion as you once did? I'm going to have a child—*yours*. Do you hear?—*do* you—?'

Yes, often I was near to the outburst, but the words never left my lips. He wouldn't know what I was talking about, and I was gradually beginning to think that if he did, he wouldn't

230

care.

If it hadn't been for the child day by day developing healthily within me, I'd have been unbearably lonely. The dark flame in Rupert's eyes sometimes—a haunted, brooding look on his haggard face—almost savage—made me believe his personality must be dual and that two beings lived beneath his forbidding exterior. One the man, stern but warm and kindly whom I knew so well, the other cold and aggressive, akin to the wild elements of moors and raging winds and sea that tore the coasts.

One afternoon when I was not needed at the house I decided to take a walk to Tregonnis. I needed fresh air and a change from the smothering doom-like atmosphere of Kerrysmoor. The weather was fresh, but not cold. I thought longingly of the spring that should soon come, trying to ignore the knowledge that it would probably mean my parting from Rupert and that part of my life forever.

As I walked down the lane to the road curving beneath Rosecarrion I had a queer feeling I was on a farewell visit—a goodbye to the many pleasant and exciting days I'd spent at the cottage, where my true involvement with Rupert had had its beginnings. And to Dame Jenny, the quaint old lady who'd once been such a vital part of my existence, but who now, since her stroke and the holocaust at Kerrysmoor had lain lifeless in her room, and did not often recognise me. There was also something else in my mind—a sense of Nemesis—of being drawn to the cottage by a purpose hidden from me, but of vital importance. When I rounded the bend of the hill, my pace quickened, I hurried on, light-footed, almost running, until I reached the place where once the gate had been, and where the charred remains of Kerrysmoor were still humped in a darkened lump.

Fresh undergrowth was beginning to sprout pale green in haphazard patches. I stood for a few moments staring at the scene where a few birds pecked among the stones. All was clear and very distinct under the pale blue sky. The fresh breeze which had met me on my way from Kerrysmoor, was now still, sheltered by the shape of the great hill. The only sound was the faint trickle of a stream from nearby, and I remember there had been one curving past the pool. What a strange, fey-like atmosphere there'd been about the pool. I wondered if it was still there, and decided to look.

Holding my cape and skirt above my ankles, I picked my way carefully through stones and rubble to where the back of the cottage had stood and where Dame Jenny's roses once bloomed so profusely. Ahead of me I saw the silver glint of water through the charred branches of willow and rock. At the time of the fire it would probably have receded into the general rubble, but when I drew close I realised with a start of surprise, the ground had reverted to a semblance of its original shape, forming a shallow dip where once silver and gold fish had darted and lilies spread their fan-like leaves. There was little water left there now, but the frail spring sunlight gave it brilliance, and as I stared a flash of silver light made me suddenly blink and shut my eyes. When I opened them I noticed something lying at one side of the quivering water.

I went forward, and picked it up, gazing in bewilderment. It was a delicate box made of mother-of-pearl, and shaped exquisitely into the form of a heart. One of the lost treasures of Tregonnis? But no. I had never seen it in the locked room. Could it have belonged to her? Melissa?

Trembling slightly I examined it—it wasn't damaged at all, or even rusted. The lid fitted perfectly; a small quantity of soil clung to it, but that was all. Either it had lain hidden for a period of time, buried perhaps beneath a stone, or it had been impervious to erosion by water or the elements.

I opened the lid carefully. What I saw inside took my breath away. The velvet lining was damp and one corner faintly mildewed. But a perfectly carved profile of a man's head in ivory—a miniature without a frame—stared up at me—the unmistakable likeness of Rupert, at an earlier age. I fingered the shining surface, took a lawn handkerchief from the pocket of my skirt, and rubbed it free of moisture. Then I turned it over and saw engraved in fine script writing on the back, 'To Melissa, with love. Rupert.'

An aching sense of nostalgia tinged with— not jealousy—but painful envy, swept over me. So he *had* loved her. Melissa, indeed, must be beyond doubt, the girl in the portrait—the girl his tortured memory had turned to when he'd begged her to understand why he'd married Alicia. At that moment I didn't seem to fit in anywhere in his life, except as a means to forgetting, —a sort of passionate compensation for the one he'd either lost or renounced. And now, through the accident, I wasn't even that.

How long I stood gazing at the memento lying in my palm I never knew. I was about to replace it near the water when I changed my mind, and decided to take it with me to Kerrysmoor. Even if it belonged to the past, it was also Rupert's property—something that must once have meant a great deal to him. Perhaps in finding and returning it, I might gain a little gratitude and warmth. I would carefully choose what I considered a propitious moment to bring it out, at a time when he appeared free of bitterness and out of pain. Such occasions were rare, but each day now his leg appeared to be easing. He walked more, and seemed on the whole less self-centred. On the other hand I could show it to

Mrs Treen and ask her advice. She might, under the circumstances, confide what she knew of Melissa.

I was so deep in thought over the problem that I didn't hear the tread of heavy footsteps over the uneven ground. The first intimation I had of anyone else's presence was the crackling of undergrowth and sound of a stone being dislodged.

Startled, I turned my head quickly and to my astonishment saw Rupert standing only a few yards away. He was staring at me intently, with no smile on his lips, no trace of warmth or pleasure at finding me there, only a grim curiosity holding, I fancied, a hint of censure. He was bare-headed, wearing a caped greatcoat. One hand rested on a gold-knobbed walking stick, as support, I supposed, for the maimed leg.

There was a pause of some seconds between us before he spoke.

'What are you doing here?'

'*Me*?—I—I've been for a walk. I wanted fresh air, and I—I found this—' I held up the box for him to see. He glanced at it, frowning—a frown that gradually gave place to bewilderment.

'Where? Where did it come from?'

'It was on the ground, near the pool,' I told him. 'It could have lain in the water, but I'm not sure. It must have been yours once, and you—you gave it, I suppose, to Melissa.'

'Melissa?' The way he spoke her name told me nothing.

'Yes.' I opened the box and pushed it towards him. 'Read it,' I continued. 'Look at the back.'

As though in a daze he propped his stick against the withered trunk of a willow, and accepted the memento with both hands. I watched his face anxiously, as he studied it, trying to follow any changing expression betraying inner emotion. There was none. Then, slowly he raised his head, and stared hard into my eyes, as though searching my very soul.

'I thought *you* were Melissa,' he said at last. 'I thought—oh God in heaven! What's happening to me? And who are *you*? Tell me, for the sake of any sanity I have left.'

'You don't remember what happened, do you?' I said, keeping my voice as gentle as possible. 'Nothing except that you once loved someone very much—'

'I know I had a fall,' he said, 'from my horse. It was when I returned from the Crimea—the war. Yes, I remember that, but afterwards— You're right of course, everything's a jumble. Even Melissa—if she ever existed.'

'I'm sure she did exist, Rupert,' I told him calmly. 'She was the girl in the portrait—the one that used to hang in your treasure room here, at the cottage, Tregonnis, before it was burned down.'

He eased himself on to a tumbled granite slab and sat there with his head in his hands, the bad leg stretched out straight before him. For that brief interim all the desire and longing in me for him turned to compassion—a deep need to comfort, and reassure. I suppose love has many sides to it, and I'd never quite experienced this overwhelming forgetfulness of self before.

I stretched out a hand. 'Rupert—' I said.

He looked up enquiringly. 'Yes? What else have you to explain? You call me Rupert instead of Mr Verne or the Master. What *am* I to you? All these weeks—I recall it now— you've been Melissa. Now, suddenly, I'm confronted by a lie, some fantastic story, about Melissa dying.'

'No,' I corrected him firmly. 'I never said Melissa died. *You* did. At least that's what you believe, obviously. You must have known her—loved her, a long time ago. Look at the miniature again, your head. You were a young man, Rupert, and Melissa must have been young too. Doesn't that tell you anything?'

He got to his feet, and reached for his stick. 'No. And this conversation leads nowhere, proves nothing, except I've lost my mind.' He regarded me closely, with a rising angry despair on his face, and when I said nothing, he continued, 'So shall we end this ridiculous conversation? I've no heart for play-acting. Here—' he thrust the box at me—'take this

237

thing. It's of no use to me. Put it back where you found it or wear it close to your heart. I don't care. I care for nothing at all. You understand?'

The cruel words inflamed and hurt me. As he turned in an effort to find his way back to the lane, I rushed after him and clutched his coat. 'No, I *don't* understand,' I shouted, 'I know it's miserable for you losing your memory and being in pain, but what about *me*?' I broke off breathlessly for a moment. 'As you don't recall anything about me I'll tell you. I'm Josephine. Josephine Lebrun, and before this awful landslide we were lovers. It was after you heard me singing at the Golden Bird in Falmouth, you brought me here and sent me to have lessons from Signor Luigi in Truro. Then we fell in love. And—and I'm going to have your baby. Can you take *that* in? It's true. A *child. Yours.*'

He spun round. His eyes were blazing. I noticed that his hand trembled on the stick. Whether he believed me or not I couldn't tell. The expression on his grim face told me nothing.

Fear, the sudden knowledge that my speech might have shocked and in some way harmed him, made me draw away, step backwards, and as I did so one of my feet, the heel of a boot, caught something—some projection entangled in the furze. I lost my balance, tried to retrieve it, but failed and pitched to the ground,

238

tumbling over the broken prone statue that had once overlooked the pool, and rolled.

As I hit the water I heard Rupert's cry of, 'No, oh *no*. Melissa?' then—'Josie—*Josie*—'

I clutched through the strangling weeds and water, struggling blindly for support as muddy slime clouded my eyes. There was no danger of drowning once I could get a foothold. The pool was shallow. But it seemed some dark deadly power was sucking all energy from my heavy body.

In those few instants I was aware of only one thing—the necessity somehow to protect the young life I carried, the fruit of our love, Rupert's and mine. I gasped for air, forced myself up, reached for the bank, and fell again, face down. Somehow I pushed my head up, and it was then I felt a strong hand gripping an arm, pulling me firmly to safety.

I lay with my chest heaving, heart pumping against my ribs while Rupert wiped my face and dripping hair. 'Oh Josie—Josie—' I heard him saying as though from a dream, 'I'm so sorry. Darling, darling—don't fret, be still. It's all over now. I *remember*. It was when you fell—And the baby—the shock of it all—'

I tried to speak, but he silenced me.

'Hush. Don't say anything. We'll talk later. My poor love, the first thing to do is get you back. Lie still now, that's a command, d'you hear? I'll get the man. He's waiting in the lane with the carriage. He'll help us.'

I smiled, though the gesture must have been a travesty, with mud still all over me.

'I must look awful,' I said feebly.

And then he too, gave the lopsided half-grin I knew so well—the first I'd seen for months.

'You do, my love. Quite a mess. A wonder I can bring myself to kiss you.'

But he did, and a minute later was escorting me over the brown earth to the lane. He hardly limped at all, and when he ushered me into the waiting carriage, his eyes were alight. It was only when we reached Kerrysmoor that reality seemed to register with either of us. I knew then that there was still a deal of explanation to follow, but whatever it might reveal, everything was well with Rupert and myself.

CHAPTER THIRTEEN

Mrs Treen was shocked when she saw the two of us enter the hall at Kerrysmoor.

'My dear soul!' she exclaimed, throwing up her hands, 'What a sight you do look—oh, not *you*, Master—but *her*, the girl. What mischief's been going on? I think I've a right to know seeing that you're supposed to be kept quiet, sir, and not be bothered by any flibbertigibbet maid who doesn't seem capable of knowing her place or where she's allowed to be and where not. I tell you, Master—it's getting me down these days—one shock after another. I do my best to run the house in a normal fashion. But how can I, I ask you? What with fires and landslides, and her ladyship going queer and dying—and now this Josephine—this French miss appearing like a drowned rat—look at the floor, all spattered up again. And that funny old Dame Jenny upstairs—full of omens she is again. It's too much—just too much—'

Rupert let the spate of words tumble out, making no attempt to stop her. When at last, with a great sigh it was done, and Mrs Treen, after a gasp, drew out a handkerchief and rubbed her nose and eyes, he said soothingly:

'I can understand. It's been very difficult for you. But things will be easier for you from now on, so calm yourself. Relax woman.' He took her arm and urged her quietly but forcibly to the parlour. 'Now sit down, and have something to liven you up.' He went to the cabinet, brought out three glasses and a decanter, and proceeded to pour three drinks. When I'd had mine which I quickly swallowed, he said, 'You'd better go and change into dry clothes, Josephine. Leave me with Mrs Treen to do a little explaining. And when you come down, see that the end of your chin and nose are clean. You *do* look rather—spectacular. It might be advisable to have a bath.'

'Thank you so much for your advice, sir,' I said, with a mockery equal to his own. 'I'll bear it in mind.'

I gave the semblance of a curtsey, then rushed from the room, and up the stairs, but not before I heard Mrs Treen saying in outraged tones, 'To think of it! —the *impertinence.*'

I didn't hear whether Rupert replied or not, neither did I really care. Happiness was bubbling up in me, in spite of my wet clothes, dripping hair, and bruises and scratches which were starting to smart.

However, when I looked into my mirror a little of my elation vanished. I was indeed a sight, and could have been some bedraggled beggar-woman or gypsy from the slums of Falmouth's dockland. Yet Rupert hadn't seemed to mind. Was it because he loved me so much or because he didn't really care? It was odd how one mood could so quickly follow upon another. But maybe exhaustion combined with my condition accounted for the creeping heaviness that gradually overcame my body.

I felt my stomach tentatively, wondering if any harm could have been done by my fall into the pool. No pain registered there, so I guessed I was all right, and proceeded to undress, for washing and perfuming myself. It was important to me, oh terribly important that when Rupert saw me I should be looking my best and most desirous—even though I might have to be uncomfortable in corsets, and somehow disguise my increasing plumpness.

He'd been pleased about the baby, which had shocked his mind alive, yes. But men were queer creatures when it came to a woman's looks, and not always reasonable about cause and effect.

Although my news concerning the child combined with the shock of seeing me tumble, had so miraculously restored his past, I couldn't be sure yet to what extent or how permanent it would be. There might be blanks which would return and thrust him back into the torment of doubt. This mustn't happen. He knew me again now as Josie, and must never for a moment be allowed to forget the fact. I must so dazzle and delight him, that all the rest—the unhappiness and perhaps tragedies he'd had to endure—would fade into shadow and eventual forgetfulness.

Of course, I was being extremely optimistic, but the joys of loving can be irrational, and when I made my way some time later along the landing towards the stairs, my heart was beating wildly; even through the film of rice powder on my cheeks, I was aware my skin must have a radiant glow. I was wearing the best dress I had—soft blue silk, trimmed with small blue velvet bows and a white lace collar and cuffs. I had no time to dry my hair properly or arrange it in an elegant fashion, but left my dark front curls to fall to my shoulders, and caught the back portion of hair up, with a blue ribbon.

I had to pass the door of Dame Jenny's room near the head of the stairs, and paused for a moment thinking I heard a thin high call. I looked in quietly. She was lying in a huge four-poster bed under a pink silk canopy with hangings to match. She could hardly move, poor old thing, but was clad in her usual fancy manner, with her bright small eyes peeping inquisitively under a frilly lace cap like a perky robin. Her bed-jacket also was ornate and fluffy, twinkling with necklaces and jewels. It must take considerable time for Mrs Treen or the girl to have her looking like that every day, I thought as I approached the bed, and the whole room must take a deal of dusting. It contained a number of ornaments, and a crystal bird swinging in a gilt cage near the window, occasionally broke with a twittering sound, into brief song.

The old lady was obviously pleased to see me. A little smile twitched her lips. She made a very slight beckoning movement of her head. I bent down towards her. A spray of rosemary lay on the quilt near her withered hand. From vague words and whispering I gathered that she meant me to have it, and remembered that she had once told me how rosemary placed under a maid's pillow at a certain time of the moon ensured happiness in love. I took it, and her smile widened. Before I had time to brush her cheek with my lips, her eyes closed, and she was asleep.

I left the room, quietly closing the door behind me, and went downstairs. Outside the parlour I waited and listened. All was quiet, so very cautiously I tapped the door, and heard Rupert's voice saying, 'Come in.'

I entered. He was alone, standing by the fireplace. I hadn't realised until then how—despite my buoyancy and exhilaration at the mere thought of contact again—apprehension and anxiety still lingered. Just inside the door I paused, wondering if I'd be disappointed, recalling other times in the past when his mood had suddenly changed from one of loving endearments to the chilly politeness of a stranger. He didn't appear unduly tired. His expression was reflective and thoughtful, until a flame from a glowing log caught his eyes lighting them to blazing gold.

'Come here, Josephine,' he said, stretching an arm towards me. 'You look quite—ravishing.'

'I hope my face is clean,' I remarked stupidly, trying for the moment to keep the conversation in a light tone, I felt so nervous. 'It got a good scrub.'

I smoothed a curl from one temple, and striving to appear dignified took two steps in his direction. Then, suddenly determination crumbled, my poise was shattered, and I ran the rest of the way straight into his arms.

When the first passionate embrace was over, but still holding me close, he led me to the sofa,

245

laid me down gently, and half seated on the edge, bent over and once more kissed me, uttering the endearments I'd ached to hear for so long a time. He paused briefly at intervals to smooth the hair from my forehead, his hands tracing the outline of my face—from temples, over cheeks and jaw, then travelling tenderly over curve of breasts. And all the while I was whispering, 'I love you so. Oh, Rupert—I do love you—'

'And I—' he whispered, 'for ever and ever—' A hand rested gently on the swelling curve of my stomach beneath the blue silk, and it was as though sensing the touch of love the unborn baby stirred in response.

'When will it be?' he asked presently. 'The birth?'

'Some time in April,' I told him, 'the spring.'

He stared at me thoughtfully before saying, 'Poor little devil! With a cripple for a father!'

'You're *not* a cripple,' I said indignantly, 'and you don't know it will be a boy. We could easily have a daughter.'

'Of course. And what would we call her?'

On impulse I said, 'Melissa, if you like; I wouldn't *mind*. Truly.'

'Ah! —Melissa. I'll have to explain about her, I suppose.'

'Only when you want to,' I answered. 'She doesn't—she doesn't seem so important any more.'

'Oh but she *is* important—very,' he said.

'She was the beginning of it all—many years ago, when we were both children. In her way she was the loveliest creature I'd ever known—until now.'

He was gazing at me so intently I looked away. A hand sought mine and pressed it. I could feel the warm pulse beating—almost as quickly as my own heart. I almost asked, Who *was* she? Is she alive still somewhere? Or did she die? But I bit my lips to keep the words back, leaving him to admit of his own accord.

'Yes, as you said earlier, I loved her. She was the daughter of our housekeeper at the time, in my father's day, so you could say we grew up together. My mother had died when I was very young, and Mrs Pendrake in most ways took her place in my life. When we were older—I was in my twenties, I determined to marry Melissa who returned my—passion. It was a young passion, but nonetheless sincere and overwhelming. But in the end—'

'Yes, Rupert?' I urged, 'what happened? Wouldn't your father agree? Was that it?'

'My father by then was dead,' he said, in colder tones. 'I doubt he knew about the affair. We'd been wise and kept our affection as secret as possible. It was only after his death that Lucas, my elder brother let out the truth—maliciously, mockingly, because unfortunately he was that type of man. Lascivious—brutal in his fashion.'

There was a pause, after which I said, 'Please

247

go on.'

'Following the funeral, and after the will was read,' Rupert continued, 'when I told him of my decision to marry Melissa, he informed me casually, but with a particularly nasty triumphant note in his voice that I couldn't because she was my own half sister—the daughter of my father—his bastard, by Mrs Pendrake. I shall never forget his words. "My dear fellow, I'm so infernally sorry. She's certainly a tasty little piece. But incest is not regarded favourably by the law, as you must know. A shame. But never mind, when you've grown up some more, you're sure to find some eligible filly to satisfy your sexual and romantic needs". I lunged out and only missed him by a quarter of an inch; and he laughed, blast him, laughed and walked away, swaggering as though he'd played an extremely clever trick—and won.'

'Was it true, though? About Melissa?'

'Being my half-sister? Oh, yes. When I confronted her, Mrs Pendrake admitted it.' He closed his eyes for a second as though to blot out that faraway scene. When he opened them again he was staring straight ahead expressionlessly. I waited for him to take up the story. 'There was proof enough in many ways,' he went on at last, 'There was no question at all that Lucas had lied. He'd known the truth since he was a youth. I think he rather revelled in it, it gave him a subtle sort of hold—or maybe equality's a better word—over my father. Neither had a scrap of conscience concerning women. They were, shall we say—of the same ilk.'

There was contempt in his voice, 'Well, the upshot of it was that Lucas inherited the greater part of the estate, and from the first moment proceeded to enjoy it. At the same time Mrs Pendrake went sick and died, she was never robust—leaving Melissa alone and unprovided for. Now the secret of her birth had become common knowledge round the immediate district, it seemed wiser under the circumstances—for her to live elsewhere, a little further out of Lucas's orbit; my father had left a certain sum to me, with a portion of land, —the cottage Tregonnis. The Crimean war was still raging; I felt I had to be there, not only because of duty, but because of the pain caused by my broken relationship with Melissa. I had to get away, somehow try to forget, for her sake as well as mine. So I arranged for her to live there with a companion—the daughter of a farmer from Penjust way. She seemed a reliable girl, better educated than most of her class. When I told Lucas he sneeringly agreed. He may have had his eye on Melissa in a certain way, but he certainly didn't *like* her; despite her looks, which he'd have ravished without a qualm given a chance, —her 'prudishness' as he termed it, got on his nerves, and irritated him.

249

So to Tregonnis Melissa and the girl went.'

There was a long pause.

'Go on, Rupert, tell me,' I said at last. 'What happened?'

'I was away for a year,' he said. 'During that time the young woman, the farmer's daughter, got married, leaving Melissa alone and unprotected. Oh, she had her weaving and spinning, kept a few fowls and goats. And the few natives round about respected her. But Lucas, seeing his chance of revenging himself on a girl who'd spurned him, proceeded to do it in his usual blackguardedly way. He called one evening and raped her. Yes. That's what the heir and owner of Kerrysmoor did, with the result that later she found herself with child.'

His voice was bitter. Even now after so long, the knuckles of one hand showed white on his clenched fist. The jaws tightened in his lean face. I didn't speak. Trite words like—'how dreadful' or 'Rupert, how simply terrible', would have been a travesty, and of no use at all. Gradually his tension eased, and he said in matter-of-fact tones, 'It was too much for her of course. What exactly happened no one exactly knew; Lucas was thrown from a horse one day after a mad gallop over the moors and was killed. I returned when I heard, and it was then I discovered that Melissa, too, was dead, drowned in the pool at the back of Tregonnis. Whether by her own hand, mischance or deliberately murdered will never be known. I suggest the latter, because I knew Lucas so well. Anyway—' he took a deep breath, '—that's the history, in brief.'

'And the portrait?'

'I'd had that painted by a good friend of mine earlier—an artist from London who came to Kerrysmoor occasionally for a visit. Later, following Melissa's death, I had it framed and hung in that small room among certain other precious relics. The place became through the years almost sacred to me—a shrine. Anything of particular beauty I could purchase, I bought and had installed there. Oh, yes, I must admit it, my love, I adored Melissa with a youthful infatuation that only seemed to increase with time—until I met you.'

'Maybe you still do, in a—in a dream-like kind of way,' I suggested wistfully, with faint pain gnawing me.

'As one admires anything that is beautiful and true,' he agreed. 'Apple blossom against a pale blue summer sky—the golden fire of summer sunset tipping the hills and passing clouds with flame—great art, and chords of forgotten music played on distant violins— oh—Josie, Josie—don't make me sound a sentimental fool. I'm an adventurer and smuggler, remember? An unscrupulous character who's defrauded the law and married a mad woman—not that I knew that at the time—to gain my own ends and get the estate on its feet again. Lucas had played merry hell

251

with Kerrysmoor, and there were debts to face I'd never have met if it hadn't been for a bit of sharp practice on my part. When Alicia came along, highly born, apparently rich and besotted with me, I'd no scruples in using her. I'd no personal illusions—I knew what I was doing, or *thought* I did. As it happened, she wasn't quite so rich as I'd believed, and the greater part of what she'd had was spent for her own comforts and apartment in the best wing.

'From the beginning our marriage was a travesty, one founded on my own bitterness and fanatical heartache, and her insatiable craving for a husband. I knew nothing of her family's taint—of the inherent insanity which eventually flared up and made her destroy Tregonnis. Jealousy! It can be a very evil thing. She would have destroyed *you* if she could; that's why I arranged for you to stay at the Crown in Truro. But you didn't trust me, did you? You merely decided I was throwing my weight about showing who was master.'

'No.' I told him. 'Not exactly. It looked rather as though you were trying to get me out of the way.'

'So I was. With Alicia escaped and on the warpath, it was the only sensible thing to do. Good heavens, Josie, she might have *killed* you. She had a knife, did you know that?'

'Yes,' I said, and I related then the sordid frightening episode when I'd been attacked in the garden of the cottage.

He sighed. 'You should have let them know at the farm. They'd have somehow managed to contact me, or the servants at Kerrysmoor.'

I didn't tell him I'd told Jan, but that he was too scared to spread the news in case he was blamed for gossiping about her ladyship. Instead, I merely remarked, 'Can't we try and forget about it all now? Oh, Rupert, shouldn't we just be thankful to be alive, and together— and—and—'

'Yes?'

'Couldn't we—couldn't you give up the other thing—the smuggling?'

'For the time being, with this wretched leg, I have to,' he answered. 'But the house is going to cost a good deal getting into order, and when we're married—'

'*When?*' I remarked pertly, 'I never said I *would* marry you, did I? How could I, you've not asked me yet.'

He paused before taking my chin in his hand and turning my face up to his. Then, before kissing me, he said whimsically with mock politeness, 'Dear Miss Lebrun, I should be most honoured if you would consent to becoming my wife.' His voice was restrained and formal, but laughter lit his golden eyes, laughter and all the love I'd hoped to find some day from this one man in the world to whom I knew I could be totally committed.

'Of course,' I said. 'Oh, Rupert—Rupert—I do love you so.'

'And I you—forever.'

From outside came the high sweet trilling of a bird. One day maybe I would also sing again. Whether or not was unimportant to me just then. We had our whole life together ahead, and spring seemed everywhere.

* * *

Our son was born on a day when the lanes and hedgerows foamed with wild cherry blossom and gorse flamed gold over the high moors. From the distance a cuckoo called; the newly laid gardens of Kerrysmoor were already starred with primroses, and the thrusting speared heads of bluebells. We called the baby Pierre Rupert—which I guessed would naturally become shortened to Piers. He was a lusty, laughing, strong-willed child, whose greenish eyes soon changed to sparkling amber. Dame Jenny, who had made a miraculous half-recovery from her stroke, insisted on placing one of her well-known lucky herbs under his pillow for the first week of his life. 'T' guard'en against witches an' pellars and the evil doings of smugglin',' she said. There was no need for the latter precaution; due to the intricate and numerous underground tunnelling of the moor behind the house, the ground had completely caved in, and been levelled not only by Rupert's men, but by Nature.

'Still, maybe it's for the best,' Rupert said a little ruefully, 'With this damned leg of mine, and you to control, my wilful love, I shall have enough to do without further adventure.'

Which proved to be perfectly true.

We hope you have enjoyed this Large Print book. Other Chivers Press or Thorndike Press Large Print books are available at your library or directly from the publishers. For more information about current and forthcoming titles, please call or write, without obligation, to:

Chivers Press Limited
Windsor Bridge Road
Bath BA2 3AX
England
Tel. (01225) 335336

OR

Thorndike Press
P.O. Box 159
Thorndike, Maine 04986
USA
Tel. (800) 223–6121 (U.S. & Canada)
In Maine call collect: (207) 948–2962

All our Large Print titles are designed for easy reading, and all our books are made to last.